New *&* Selected

Poems

1957–2011

ALSO BY ROBERT SWARD

BOOKS OF POETRY
- *Advertisements, Odyssey Chapbook Number One, 1958*
- *Uncle Dog & Other Poems,* 1962
- *Kissing The Dancer & Other Poems,* Introduction by William Meredith, 1964
- *Thousand-Year-Old Fiancée,* 1965
- *Horgbortom Stringbottom, I Am Yours, You Are History,* 1970
- *Hannah's Cartoon,* 1970
- *Quorum/Noah* (With Mike Doyle), 1970
- *Gift,* 1971
- *Five Iowa Poems,* 1975
- *Cheers For Muktananda,* 1976
- *Honey Bear On Lasqueti Island, B.C.,* 1978
- *Six Poems,* 1980
- *Twelve Poems,* 1982
- *Movies: Left To Right,* 1983
- *Half-A-Life's History, Poems New & Selected,* Introduction by Earle Birney, 1983
- *The Three Roberts, Premiere Performance,* 1984 Featuring Robert Priest, Robert Zend and Robert Sward
- *The Three Roberts On Love,* 1985
- *The Three Roberts On Childhood,* 1985
- *Poet Santa Cruz,* Introduction by Morton Marcus, 1985
- *Four Incarnations, New & Selected Poems,* 1991
- *Rosicrucian in the Basement,* Introduction by William Minor, 2001
- *Three Dogs and a Parrot,* 2001
- *Heavenly Sex, New & Selected Poems,* 2002
- *The Collected Poems, 1957-2004* (second printing 2006)
- *God is in the Cracks,* 2006 (second printing 2007)

FICTION
- *The Jurassic Shales, A Novel,* 1975
- *Family,* with contributions by David Swanger, Charles Atkinson, Tilly Shaw, 1994
- *A Much-Married Man, A Novel,* 1996

NON-FICTION
- *The Toronto Islands,* An Illustrated History, 1983
- *Autobiography,* Contemporary Authors Autobiography Series (CAAS), Vol. 206, 2003

EDITED BY ROBERT SWARD
- *Vancouver Island Poems,* An Anthology, 1973
- *Emily Carr: The Untold Story,* 1978

CDS, DVDS, ELECTRONIC BROADSIDES AND CHAPBOOKS
- *Rosicrucian in the Basement,* as read by the author, Recorded for the KPFA-FM Program: *Cover to Cover,* Berkeley, CA, 2002
- *Robert Sward: Poetry, Review & Interview with Jack Foley,* Recorded for the KPFA-FM Program: *Cover to Cover,* Berkeley, CA, 2002
- *Writers' Friendship, A conversation with Jack Foley and Robert Sward,* Recorded for the KPFA-FM Program: *Cover to Cover,* Berkeley, CA, 2003
- *Robert Sward Interview for 'The Muse' DVD Magazine,* Boss Productions, DVD Video, 2005.
- *The Dogs in My Life,* Blue's Cruzio Café, DVD, 2008.
- *DVD Muse Magazine,* produced and edited by Wallace Boss, Santa Cruz, CA, 2005 wboss@sbcglobal.net
- *Earthquake Collage,* Blue Moon Review, electronic chapbook based on 1989 Loma Prieta earthquake
- *God is in the Cracks,* electronic chapbook, mp3 sound, graphics, seven poems read by the author—found on the following websites: http://www.robertsward.com http://jjwebb.ihwy.com/rosycrossfather/index.html

Video component of the electronic chapbook: http://www.VirtualWorldStudio.com

- *A Man Needs A Place to Stand*—One-minute autobiographical poem—A Future Peak video found on the following website: http://www.futurepeak.net/vidlinks/robertswardstand2005.htm

New & Selected

Poems

1957–2011

Robert Sward

RED HEN PRESS | *Pasadena, CA*

New & Selected Poems: 1957–2011

Copyright © 2011 by Robert Sward

Book design by Andrew Mendez

ISBN: 978-1-59709-261-6 (tradepaper)
ISBN: 978-1-59709-453-5 (hardcover)

Library of Congress Cataloging-in-Publication Data
Sward, Robert, 1933–
 [Poems. Selections]
 New & selected poems, 1957–2011 / Robert Sward.
   p. cm.
 ISBN 978-1-59709-261-6 (tradepaper)
 I. Title. II. Title: New and selected poems, 1957–2011.
 PS3569.W3A6 2011
 811'.54—dc22

                    2011020510

The Los Angeles County Arts Commission, the California Arts Council, the National Endowment for the Arts, and City of Los Angeles Department of Cultural Affairs partially support Red Hen Press.

First Edition
Published by Red Hen Press
www.redhen.org

ACKNOWLEDGMENTS

Grateful acknowledgment is made to the editors of the following publications for permission to reprint many of the poems in this book:

Arion 9 (Buenos Aires, Argentina), *Alsop Review* (eZine), *Ambit* (London), *Another Chicago Magazine* (ACM #37), *Antioch Review, Approach Magazine, Arts in Society* (Madison, Wisconsin), *The Activist* (Oberlin College), *Artes/Letres Dialogos* (Mexico City), *Beloit Poetry Journal, Best Articles & Stories, Blue Moon Review* (eZine), *BookPress: The Newspaper of the Literary Arts* (Ithaca, NY), *Carleton Miscellany, Center* (New York), *Chelsea Review* (New York), *Chicago Review, Contemporary Verse II* (University of Manitoba, Canada), *Cross Canada Writers' Quarterly* (Toronto), *Davka, Jewish Cultural Revolution DAVKA,* (San Francisco), *Denver Quarterly, Descant, Disquieting Muses* (eZine), *El Corno Emplumado* (Mexico City), *Epoch* (Cornell University), *The Etruscan* (New South Wales, Australia), *Exposicion Exhaustiva De La Nueva Poesia Galeria* (Montevideo, Uruguay), *Equal Time* (New York); *Extensions* (New York), *Fiction-Online, An Internet Literary Magazine, The Fiddlehead* (New Brunswick, Canada), *From A Window* (Tucson, AZ), *Galley Sail Review, Greenfield Review* (Greenfield Center, NY), *Hanging Loose Press* (Brooklyn, NY), *Hawaii Review* (Honolulu), *Hudson Review, The Humanist, Inkstone* (Bowling Green, Ohio), *The Iowa Review, Karaki* (Victoria, B.C.), *Kayak* (Santa Cruz, CA), *Malahat Review* (Victoria, B.C.), *The Martlet* (Victoria, B.C.), *Massachusetts Review, Matrix,* (London, England), *Michigan Quarterly Review, Mt. Shasta Selections* (MSS*), Monterey Bay Poetry Festival 2003 Chapbook* (Monterey, CA), *Mudlark, An Electronic Journal of Poetry & Poetics* (eZine), *Mudlark Poster #7, The Nation, New Mexico Quarterly, New Orleans Poetry Journal, New Work #1, The New Yorker, The New York Times, The North American Review, Northern Light* (University of Manitoba), *The Northstone Review* (Minneapolis, MN), *Octavo, The Paris Review, Pearl* (Denmark), *Penny Poems, Perspective* (St. Louis, MO), *Poetry* (Chicago), *Poetry Magazine.com* (eZine), *Poetry Toronto, Poetry Australia, Poetry Northwest, Prism International* (Vancouver, B.C.), *Psychological Perspectives, A Journal of Jungian Thought, Quarterly Review of Literature, Rampike* (York University, Canada), *Realpoetik* (Rpoetik, eZine), *Salt Spring Island Tatler* (eZine), *Santa Clara Review* (Santa Clara University, CA), *The Santa Cruz Sentinel, Santa Cruz Weekly, Shenandoah, Stone* (Ithaca, NY), *Signal Hill Broadsides* (Victoria, B.C.), *Shirim* (A Jewish Poetry Journal), *Tambourine* (St. Louis, MO), *Transatlantic Review* (London, England), *Tri-Quarterly* (Evanston, IL), *Tuatara* (Victoria, B.C.), *UCSC Student Guide* (Santa Cruz, CA), *Waves* (Toronto), *Web Del Sol* (eZine),

Literary Art on the World Wide Web, *West Coast Works* (Vancouver, B.C.), *Wild Dog*, *X-Connect* (CrossConnect), *Zahir* (Portsmouth, NH).

Some of these poems have been recorded by Western Michigan University's Aural Press (1005); the Library of Congress; National Public Radio (New Letters On The Air, University of Missouri); KPFA-FM (Berkeley, CA); and Uncle Dog Audio.

CDs include *Rosicrucian in the Basement, Read by the Author*, Uncle Dog Audio 1001 and *Robert Sward: Poetry, Review & Interview, with Jack Foley*, Uncle Dog Audio 1002. Anthologized work: *A Controversy Of Poets, An Anthology Of Contemporary American Poets; Bear Flag Republic: Prose Poems and Poetics from California; The Chicago Review Anthology; The Contemporary American Poets: American Poetry Since 1940; A Cure Within: A History of Mind-Body Medicine; Heartland: Poets Of The Midwest; Inside Outer Space; New Poems of The Space Age; Illinois Poetry; Inventions For Imaginative Thinking; Quarry West #35, (University of California at Santa Cruz), Anthology, Poets & Writers of Monterey Bay; Lighthouse Point: An Anthology of Santa Cruz Writers; Midland: 25 Years Of Fiction And Poetry; New Yorker Book of Poems; The Now Voices; Oxford Book Of Light Verse; Penguin Book of Animal Poetry; Riverside Poetry III; Silver Screen: Neue Amerikanische Lyrik; Some Haystacks Don't Even Have Any Needle; Sports Poems; The Practical Imagination; The Space Atlas; Stories of Our Mothers & Fathers; Tesseracts: Canadian Science Fiction; The Treasure Of Our Tongue; The Voice That Is Great Within Us; To Say The Least, Canadian Poets From A To Z; Tough Times: When The Money Doesn't Love Us; and Where Is Vietnam? American Poets Respond; X-Connect (Cross Connect), Writers of the Information Age.*

See also *Contemporary Authors, A Bio-Bibliographical Guide*, Volume 206, *2003.*

R.D. Brinkmann and Peter Behrens translated some of these poems into German in a volume titled *Silver Screen, Neue Amerikanische Lyrik*, Kiepenheuer & Witsch, Koln. Others were translated into Spanish by Madela Ezcurra and Eduwardo Costa and appeared in *AIRON* 9, Buenos Aires, Argentina.

Grateful acknowledgment is also made to the editors of the following publications or media where various of these poems were published, recorded or broadcast: *Faith and Doubt, An Anthology*, Henry Holt & Co., *Monterey Bay Poetry Review, The New Quarterly Anthology* (Canada) #95 (Special Poetry Issue), *Nimrod International Journal #27* (Awards Issue), *Passager Poetry Contest / Passager Literary Journal*, Poesy, *Rosy Cross Father* (An electronic chapbook with mp3 sound, graphics, video by Virtual World Studio, Boulder Creek, CA, and seven poems from *God is in the Cracks* including QuickTime video, *A Man Needs a Place to Stand,* Virtual World Studio and J.J. Webb / Beau Blue Presents <http://jjwebb.ihwy.com/rosycrossfather/cracks_main2.html, Writers' Almanac, National Public Radio, the poems *God is in the Cracks* and *Ode to Torpor* read by Garrison Keillor, <http://writersalmanac.publicradio.org/programs/2004/03/22/>

Gloria in Excelsis

My children and grandchildren: Cheryl, Kamala, Michael, Hannah, Nicholas–Aaron, Robin, Maxine, Heron, Fjord

* * *

With thanks to Elissa Alford, Heidi Alford, Jonathan Alford, David Alpaugh, Charles Atkinson, Ellen Bass, Rose Black, Robert Bly, Dr. Rachel Callaghan, Maria Elena Caballero-Robb, Ruth Daigon, Dion Farquhar, Jack Foley, Dana Gioia, Heidi Alford Jones, Peter Gilford, James D. Houston, Dr. Ed Jackson, Coeleen Kiebert, Allan Kornblum, John D. Lee, Patrick McCarthy, Mort Marcus, Marti Mariette, Doug McClellan, Bruce Meyer, William Minor, Neil Roberts, Tilly Shaw, David Swanger, Hannah Sward, and J.J. Webb.

My thanks also to Mark Cull and Kate Gale at Red Hen Press for their generosity and commitment to my work. To Allan Kornblum, Coffee House Press, and to Marty Gervais, Black Moss Press. And Marti Mariette, for assistance above and beyond the call of duty.

TABLE OF CONTENTS

UNCLE DOG BECOMES A BODHISATTVA
AN INTRODUCTION TO ROBERT SWARD'S WORK

Reminiscences from Cornell University, over forty years ago: I remember the eyes: large, hazel-brown, luminous, kindly. And the manner: hesitant but pleasant. And the sense one had of a gentle, oddly elegant madness. He was tall: one thought he must look like Robert Lowell. And there was insight: he would stammer, but there were always ideas, intelligence, something worth listening to. And the oddity of the poems.

Robert Sward's career began in the late 1950s. Though well-known, he is not nearly as well-known as he should be. Sward's poems are often comic, but they are rarely *only* comic—or for that matter *only* seriocomic. This poet's work is the result of a plunge into a never fully ironized, often hilarious sense of *mysticism*: It is the product of a restless, spiritually adventuresome sensibility masking itself as a stand-up comedian. "Born on the Jewish North Side of Chicago," Sward writes of himself, "bar mitzvahed, sailor, amnesiac, university professor (Cornell, Iowa, Connecticut College), newspaper editor, food reviewer, father of five children, husband to four [now five] wives. . . ."

The poet's mother died in 1948 at the age of 42; her last words were a request "to keep [Robert's] feet on the ground." And indeed, feet are an important aspect of this poet's work. Sward describes his podiatrist father as "a cross between Charlie Chaplin and Errol Flynn" as well as "ambitious and hard-working." A perfectly respectable man. By the time Sward wrote the poems collected in *Rosicrucian in the Basement*, the father has blossomed into a full-fledged eccentric, a visionary adrift in a world that doesn't comprehend him: "'There are two worlds,' [the father] says lighting incense, / 'the seen and the unseen . . . / This is my treasure.'"

It was only after Sward's mother's death that his father became "a strict and devout" Rosicrucian, but like his father, Sward "lives in another world." The poet is, however, not so certain which world that is. When the father says, "As above, so below," the son answers, "I'm not so sure." The word "below" is partly ironic since the podiatrist father is always talking about feet and because the father carries out his rituals in the basement. Yet it is also, as in Hermes Trismegistus, a serious assertion about the relationship between the world of the senses and the "other" world. Sward's own impulses led him away from both his family's Judaism and his father's Rosicrucianism. In "Prayer for My Mother," one of his most moving and accomplished poems, Sward is accused of being a "Jew who got away," a "sinner."

The young Robert Sward "was nicknamed 'Banjo Eyes,' after the singer Eddie Cantor. Friends joked about my name: 'The Sward is mightier than the Sword.' And because I had a zany imagination, I had only to say, 'Hey, I have an idea,' and other eight-year-olds would collapse laughing. I was regarded as an oddball, an outsider. I had few friends."

Robert Sward learned early that the comic, the "zany," was a mask by which one could assert oneself—through which one would be listened to. In his poems, the mask remains, but it is at the service of an essentially visionary impulse: "the vision, the life that it requires." The word "dream" haunts his work. Sward remains simultaneously "not so sure" and utterly certain: "For two, maybe three, minutes / I saw two worlds interpenetrating."

As a poet, Robert Sward inhabits an enormous in-between. It will come as no surprise to readers to find that his poems get at the moment of truth by being deeply unsettled, by refusing to rest in any particular other than the cosmic ambiguity of an area which is both wholly visionary and wholly sensual—and in which the visionary and the sensual are not resolved. Past, present and future—and their tenses—assail him equally: "As a teacher, I talk. That's present. / For thirty years as a teacher, I talked. That's past. / It may only be part time, but I will talk. That's future."

Sward's poetry has undergone many shifts—including the shift from free verse to closed forms—but its fundamental impulse seems not to have changed since I first came upon it in the early 60s. Outwardly "zany" and fanciful, it is inwardly serious, troubled and questioning. He has written over twenty books of poetry as well as some fiction and non-fiction; in the late 1980s he entered the Internet, poems a-flying. He has produced CDs. He once described himself as "a heat-seeking cocky mocky poetry missile . . . a low-down, self-involved dirty dog. Woof woof." He has noted how many of his poems have "to do with love, divorce, multiple marriage, aging, loss, and the challenge of bringing up children in a highly unstable world." He identifies strongly with strange and sometimes hostile animals.

What is sought in all this work is liberation, illumination—*it*. The joy of his writing is the joy of the quest. He is over 70 and is producing work as fine as what he was producing forty years ago. He has not grown *up* exactly, but he has grown. "These days," he says, "I'm paying more attention to Ben Franklin ['Early to bed, early to rise, makes a man healthy, wealthy and wise.'] and less to Blake with his lines about 'the road of excess.'" From beyond the grave the poet's father counsels him, "Spend some time at the Invisible College."

—Jack Foley, Berkeley/Oakland, CA

AUTHOR'S NOTE

Ram Dass says, "Old age is about harvesting whatever your life's work has been." Now in my 70's, I don't feel especially old, but my life's work has been, and continues to be, poetry, and, fifty years after my first publication, this is harvest time. From the thousand or so poems I've written since the early 1950s, these are the ones I'd like to preserve. Because it draws on some earlier collections, *Half A Life's History: New & Selected, 1957-1983*; *Four Incarnations,* and *Heavenly Sex* (among others), I have come to think of this volume as something of a 'Collected Selected.' However, I have included twenty or so new poems as well, among them the father-son series, Shelby the dog and others.

New & Selected

Poems

1957–2011

Uncle Dog

& Other Poems

1962

UNCLE DOG: THE POET AT 9

I did not want to be old Mr.
Garbage man, but uncle dog
who rode sitting beside him.

Uncle dog had always looked
to me to be truck-strong
wise-eyed, a cur-like Ford

Of a dog. I did not want
to be Mr. Garbage man because
all he had was cans to do.

Uncle dog sat there me-beside-him
emptying nothing. Barely even
looking from garbage side to side:

Like rich people in the backseats
of chauffeur-cars, only shaggy
in an unwagging tall-scrawny way.

Uncle dog belonged any just where
he sat, but old Mr. Garbage man
had to stop at every single can.

I thought. I did not want to be Mr.
Everybody calls them that first.
A dog is said, *Dog*! Or by name.

I would rather be called Rover
than Mr. And sit like a tough
smart mongrel beside a garbage man.

Uncle dog always went to places
unconcerned, without no hurry.
Independent like some leashless

Toot. Honorable among scavenger
can-picking dogs. And with a bitch
at every other can. And meat:

His for the barking. Oh, I wanted
to be uncle dog—sharp, high fox-
eared, cur-Ford truck-faced

With his pick of the bones.
A doing, truckman's dog
and not a simple child-dog

Nor friend to man, but an uncle
traveling, and to himself—
and a bitch at every second can.

THE KITE

I still heard Auntie Blue
after she did not want to come down
again. She was skypaper, way up
too high to pull down. The wind
liked her a lot, and she was lots of noise
and sky on the end of the string.
And the string jumped hard all of a sudden,
and the sky never even breathed,
but was like it always was, slow and close
far-away blue, like poor dead Uncle Blue.

Auntie Blue was gone, and I could not
think of her face. And the string fell down
slowly for a long time. I was afraid to pull it
down. Auntie Blue was in the sky,
just like God. It was not my birthday
anymore, and everybody knew, and dug
a hole, and put a stone on it
next to Uncle Blue's stone, and he died
before I was even born. And it was too bad
it was so hard to pull her down; and flowers.

DODO

The dodo is two feet high, and laughs.
A parrot, swan-sized, pig-, scale-legged
bird. Neither parrot, nor pig—nor swan.
Its beak is the beak of a parrot,
a bare-cheeked, wholly beaked and speechless
parrot. A bird incapable of
anything—but laughter. And silence:
a silence that is laughter—and fact.
And a denial of fact (and bird).
It is a sort of turkey, only
not a turkey; not anything.—Not
able to sing, not able to dance
not able to fly . . .
       —The Dutch called it the 'nauseous bird,'
Walguögel, 'the uncookable.'
Its existence (extinct as it is)
is from the Portuguese: *Duodo*, 'dumb,'
'stupid,' 'silly.' And the story of its
having been eaten on Rodrigues
Island by hogs, certain sailors & monkeys:
Didus ineptus. A bird that aided
its own digestion, of seeds and leaves,
by swallowing large stones. It has been called,
though with birds (extinct or otherwise)
crosses are a lie, a cross between
a turkey and a pigeon. The first,
it is claimed, won out; and, having won,
took flight from flight (its wings but tails, gray

yellow tufted white). And for reasons
as yet unknown.
                    Its beak is laughter
and shines, in indifference—and size.
It has the meaning, for some, of wings:
wings that have become a face: embodied
in a beak . . . and half the dodo's head . . .
It laughs—silence, its mind, extends from its ears:
its laugh, from wings, like wrists, to bill, to ears.

HELLO POEM

Hello wife, hello world, hello God,
I love you. Hello certain monsters,
ghosts, office buildings, I love you. Dog,
dog-dogs, cat, cat-cats, I love you.
Hello Things-In-Themselves, Things Not Quite
In Themselves (but trying), I love you.
River-rivers, flower-flowers, clouds
and sky;
   the Trolley Museum in Maine
(with real trolleys); airplanes taking
off; airplanes not taking off; airplanes
landing,
  I love you.

The IRT,
BMT; the London subway
(yes, yes, pedants, the Underground)
system; the Moscow subway system,
all subway systems except the
Chicago subway system. Ah yes,
I love you, the Chicago El-
evated. Sexual intercourse,
hello, hello.
  Love, I love you; Death,
I love you;
   and some other things, as well,
I love you. Like what? Walt Whitman,
   Wagner, Henry Miller;

a really
extraordinary, one-legged
Tijuana whore; I love you, loved
you.

    The *Reader's Digest* (their splendid,
monthly vocabulary tests), *Life*
and *Look* . . .

    handball, volleyball, tennis;
croquet, basketball, football, Sixty-
nine;

    draft beer for a nickel; women
who will lend you money, women
who will not;

    women, pregnant women;
women who I am making pregnant;
women who I am not making pregnant.
Women. Trees, goldfish, silverfish,
coral fish, coral;

    I love you, I
love you.

Kissing The Dancer

& Other Poems

1964

KISSING THE DANCER

Song is not singing,
   the snow

Dance is dancing,
   my love

On my knees, with voice
   I kiss her knees

And dance; my words are song,
   for her

I dance; I give up my words,
   learn wings instead

We fly like trees
   when they fly

To the moon. There, there are
   some now

The clouds opening, as you, as we
   are there

     Come in!

I love you, kiss your knees
   with words,

Enter you, your eyes
     your lips, like

          Lover
Of us all,

    words sweet words
    learn wings instead.

MARRIAGE

I lie down in darkness beside her,
this earth in a wedding gown.
        Who, what
she is, I do not know,
nor is it a question the night
would ask. I have listened—

        The woman
beside me breathes. I kiss that,
a breath or so of her, and glow.
        Glow.
Hush now, my shadow, let us . . .

Day breaks—

        depart.
Yes, and so we have.

CHICAGO'S WALDHEIM CEMETERY

We are in Chicago's Waldheim Cemetery.
I am walking with my father.
My nose, my eyes,
      left pink wrinkled oversize
      ear
my whole face is in my armpit.

We are at the stone beneath which lies
my father's mother.
There is embedded in it a pearl-shaped portrait.
I do not know this woman.
      I never saw her.
I am suddenly enraged, indignant.
I clench my fists. I would like to strike her.
My father weeps.
He is Russian. He weeps with
      conviction, sincerity, enthusiasm.
I am attentive.
I stand there listening beside him.
After a while, a little bored,
      but moved,
I decide myself to make the effort.
I have paid strict attention.
I have listened carefully.
Now, I too will attempt tears.
They are like song.
They are like flight.
I fail.

SCENES FROM A TEXT

Several actual, potentially and/or really traumatic situations are depicted on these pages.
—Transient Personality Reactions to Acute or Special Stress (Chapter 5).

Photo II

The house is burning. The furniture
is scattered on the lawn (tables, chairs
TV, refrigerator). Momma—
there is a small, superimposed white
arrow pointing at her—is busy
tearing out her eyes. The mute husband
(named, arrowed) stands idly by, his hands
upon his hips, eyes already out.
The smoke blankets the sky. And the scene,
apart from Momma, Poppa, the flames . . .
could be an auction. Friends, relatives
neighbors, all stand by, reaching, fighting
for the mirrors, TV, sunglasses;
the children, the cats and speechless dogs.

NIGHTGOWN, WIFE'S GOWN

Where do people go when they go to sleep?
I envy them. I want to go there too.
I am outside of them, married to them.
Nightgown, wife's gown, women that you look at,
beside them—I knock on their shoulder blades
ask to be let in. It is forbidden.
But you're my wife, I say. There is no reply.
Arms around her, I caress her wings.

SOCRATES AT THE SYMPOSIUM
(SONNET FOR TWO VOICES)

Of Love, my friends (after such sophistry
and praise as yours), may one presume? Well, then,
let me begin by begging Agathon:
Good sir, is not your love a love for me?
And not a love for those who disagree?
Yes, true! And what is it that Love, again,
is the love of? Speak! *It is the love again
of "Socrates."* Love then, and the Good, are me.

Explain! Is Love the love of something, or
the love of nothing? *Something!* Very true.
And Love desires the thing it loves. *Right.*
Is it, then, really me whom you adore?
Or is it nothing? *O Socrates, it's you!*
Then I am Good, and I am yours. *Agreed!*

ALL FOR A DAY

All day I have written words.
My subject has been that: Words.
And I am wrong. And the words.
      I burn
three pages of them. Words.
And the moon, moonlight, that too
I burn. A poem remains.
But in the words, in the words,
in the fire that is now words.
I eat the words that remain,
and am eaten. By nothing,
by all that I have not made.

Thousand-Year-Old Fiancée

& Other Poems

1965

MOVIES: LEFT TO RIGHT

The action runs left to right,
cavalry, the water-skiers—
then a 5-hour film, *The Sleeper*,
a man sleeping for five hours
(in fifteen sequences),
sleeping left to right, left to right
cavalry, a love scene, elephants.
Also the world goes left to right,
the moon and all the stars, sex too
and newspapers, catastrophe.

In bed, my wives are to my left.
I embrace them moving left to right.
I have lived my life that way,
growing older, moving eastward—
the speedometer, the bank balance
architecture, good music.
All that is most real moves left to right,
declares my friend the scenarist,
puffing on a white cigar, eating
The *Herald Tribune*, the *New Republic*.

My life is a vision, a mechanism
that runs from left to right. I have lived badly.
Water-skier, I was until recently
in the U.S. Cavalry. Following that
I played elephant to a lead by Tarzan.
Later, I appeared in a film called *The Sleeper*.

Till today, standing on the edge of things,
falling and about to fall asking, Why?
I look back. Nowhere. Meanwhile, one or more wives
goes on stilts for the mail.

THOUSAND-YEAR-OLD FIANCÉE

We are alone, Death's thousand-year-old fiancée
and I. The thing suggests itself to me.
I step onto the front parts of her feet,
and stand like that facing her saying nothing.
In moments I lose twenty pounds and sweat. My nose
       bleeds.
It occurs to me I may never before
have acted out of instinct. We do not embrace.
She is in her middle sixties, with varicose veins,
whitish hair and buttocks as large as Russia.
Things come off of her in waves, merriment,
exuberance, benevolent body lice,
hundred-year-old blackheads. I kiss her hives.
I lick her nose that shows she drinks bottles
and bottles of vodka every day.
I am standing there in my Jewish hair
facing her with my life. Knock, knock.
It is Death in spats and a blue business suit.
I stand there in my Jewish hair facing him.
He is very still, grinning, grayish, bemused.
Pretty soon I begin to scream. All night I scream.
Yeah. After a while I go under and kiss
her ass. It takes a bit. Fathers and sons,
I am up to my knees in the moon.
Kiss this ghost she says of a certain light.
I plunge my tongue into it to the ears. Madam,
I say, astounded, choking, feverish,
I have not as yet had you. Have me, she says.

Under my foreskin there is a star, whole
constellations. Goddammit, I am not
speaking to you here of sex! Kiss me here,
she says. Kiss me there. Stars, ghosts and sons,
                              winged,
we are all of us winged—
                    the one thing
there is of us. Death, you old lecher,
I affirm you, I confront you with my balls.
I revere dead fish and sunken submarines,
the little red schoolhouse and the American way.
Let us in fact join hands with the universe.

Death, I have news for you. I climb into
your young fiancée eleven times a night.
There are signs that she is pregnant.
Death, there is nothing I will not love.

REPORT FROM THE FRONT

All over newspapers have stopped appearing,
and combatants everywhere are returning home.
No one knows what is happening.
The generals are on long distance with the President,
Surveying the planet from on high.
No one knows even who has died, or how,
or who won last night, anything.
Those in attendance on them may,
for all we know, still be there.

All over newspapers have stopped appearing.
Words once more, more than ever,
have begun to matter. And people are writing
poetry. Opposing regiments, declares a friend,
are refusing evacuation, are engaged instead
in sonnet sequences; though they understand, he says,
the futility of iambics in the modern world.
That they are concerned with the history and meaning
of prosody. That they persist in their exercises
with great humility and reverence.

IOWA

What a strange happiness.
Sixty poets have gone off drunken, weeping into the hills,
I among them.
There is no one of us who is not a fool.
What is to be found there?
What is the point in this?
Someone scrawls six lines and says them.
What a strange happiness.

IOWA WRITERS' WORKSHOP—1958

—For Paul Engle

Seated, against the room, against the walls
legs extended, or under chairs
iambs, trochees & knees . . .
we surrender, each of us, to the sheets
at hand. The author swallows his voice. Still

"Page two." Page one is saved for the last.
"The poet has here been impressed
by the relationship
between blue birds and black. In the octet
we note the crow. And its iambic death."

"On page three, '*The Poet Upon His Wife*',
(by his wife) we note the symbols
for the poet: the bird
in flight, the collapsing crow, the blue bird . . .
Note too the resemblance between sonnets."

We vote and stare at one another's crow.
Ours is an age of light. Our crows
reflect the age, Eisenhower-Nixon
colored stripes, rainbow-solids, blacks & whites.
Ruffling their wings, Mezey, Coulette, Levine
refuse to vote.

"Page four, '*Apologies to William S.*'
apologies, our third sonnet . . ."
And those who teach, who write

and teach, the man at hand, apologize
for themselves, and themselves at hand.

"Poets buy their socks at Brooks & Warren,
like DuPont, like Edsel, like Ike."
Anecdotes, whispers, cliques
whispering, then aloud into prominence.
Brooks & Warren, DuPont, Edsel & Ike.

Order is resumed. *"We have been here, now
forever. From the beginning
of verse."* One has written
nothing, and it is inconceivable
that one would, or will ever write again.
A class has ended. They pass by, gazing
in. The poets gaze out, and grin.
They gaze out, and through the
electric voice, the ruffled sonnet sheets
that stare against the faces staring in.

"Page one." Walled-in glances at the author.
And then the author disappears,
the poem anonymous.
Voice. Voices. There are voices about it:
anonymous. The self. A sonnet's self ...

The room is filled with it. It is a bird.
It sits beside us and extends
its wings. Mezey hits it with his elbow.
The bird shrieks and sprawls
upon the floor. We surrender

We surrender to its death. The poem breathes,
becomes its author and departs.
We all depart. And watch
the green walls take our seats. Apologies.
Brooks & Warren. DuPont. Edsel & Ford.

HONEY BEAR

She is a Russian honey bear
with very strong soft brown arms.
Hugging her is at once a feat
of strength, and an act of gentle surrender.

One cannot hug the honey bear
with only half a heart. It's all
or no honey bear. There's a snap
and vibrancy to her kisses

Pucker and snap—audible
across a field of wild black
berries. Honey bear loves fresh cream
and wild berries of all kinds

French cheeses and home baked bread.
She is earth tremors in the garden,
laughter in the flower beds
rough brown honey bear pulling weeds.

Her feet, large, perfectly
            proportioned
            are powerful as
angel wings. A pale blue light
surrounds her toes as she waltzes

By the clover and the mint.
Lighter than air, heavier
than a bear. Clear-skinned lady
 O fairest of the fair

 I bow to my honey bear.

BLIND POET

—For Marcie

She has braces on her teeth and wears
a blue and orange plaid cotton shirt:

One of fourteen students

Wiggles, chatters, finds her way
into her friends' poems.

Straightens her back like a pianist
readying herself for a performance.

Sitting upright, intent
she completes, aloud,
ahead of the others

Their own, half-formed images. "Dammit, Marcie,
whose poem is this?"

They squirm, they squabble, and defer.
Composing herself,
both hands moving smoothly

Over an embossed, a Braille keyboard
of otherwise blank pages,
she reads

From a manuscript of dots. First
a lyric
she has just written

And hastily transcribed—before class—
and another,
"Wishing You Were Here"

Like a passenger waking
aboard a crowded ferryboat
on a frozen lake

My voice
lost in the voices
of the others, I cry out

"Hey, you prodigy
ferryboat Captain,
inventor in the night,

Who's writing this anyway?"

MR. AMNESIA

Even an amnesiac remembers some things
        better than others.
In one past life I was a subway conductor
for the Chicago subway system.

In another I was—Gosh, I forgot!
Anyway, some years ago, I was run over
by a sports car. Ever since that time

I find I cannot go more than a few days
without leaving my body at least briefly
and then coming back to it. Again and again.

I can't seem to stay in Chicago or in any city,
for that matter, and in one body,
for very long.

I once wrote a forty-nine-line poem
made up entirely of first lines, forty-nine beginnings.
Forty-nine Beginnings it was called.

I once met a young mother who had gone fishing
with her two children. Coming up from the bottom
of Lake Michigan, I got tangled up in their lines

And they pulled me out and saved my life.
The woman was my wife and the children were
        my children.
"Making love, it's always as if it were happening

"for the first time," I said after ten years of marriage.
"When a woman chooses an amnesiac as her husband,
  she has to expect things like that," she laughed.

"Still, there's a lot to be said
  for ten years of foreplay."
An Instructor in Modern Poetry, I once lectured

For four weeks as if each class was the first class
of a new year. When the genial Chairman,
manifesting polite alarm,

Visited my classes, the occasion of his being there
gave me the opportunity to teach
as if those classes, too, were new classes.

Promoted, given a raise, a bonus and a new two-year
                    contract,
even I was confused. Each class I taught became one
in an infinite series of semesters, each semester

Lasting no more than fifty minutes.
I don't know about you, but I hardly unpack
and get ready for this lifetime and it's time

To move on to the next. I've been reincarnated
                    three times,
and am forty-nine years old and I don't even know

              my own name.
History is just one of those things

You learn to live without. I live in a city
the entire population of which is made up of amnesiacs
so for the first time in three lifetimes I feel at home.

YADDO

I'm at Yaddo sheltering myself from the drizzle
    standing under a tree
reading Philip Roth's *The Great American Novel*
waiting for my friends Joe and Carol Bruchac
to arrive
with four friends from Canada
who are in Saratoga Springs, New York,
to give a poetry reading,
Bruce Meyer, Richard Harrison, Robert Lawrence
    and Ross Leckie,
when up pulls this big shiny car
which I approach smiling
thinking it's Joe and Carol,
but it's Burns International
    Security Services, Inc.
and the man wants to know if Yaddo
has anything more than "internal security."
    "I'm John Weidman," he says.
"You must be a writer."
"Yep."
"What's your name?"
"Sward, my name is Robert Sward, like greensward."
"Oh," he says, disappointed he doesn't
know any of my books but
still impressed to be meeting
a Yaddo author.
I should have said, "My name is
Philip Roth, John, and this is my new book,

The Great American Novel,
but as usual I think of things like that
too late.
"Look," he says, handing me his business card,
J.W. Weidman
Security Sales Consultant,
"Mention my name in your next book, okay?"

PERSONAL STRESS ASSESSMENT

(Found Poem)

Make a list of all the life events that
apply to you . . . then add them up with
the points assigned.

To be married and moderately unhappy
is less stressful than to be unmarried
and male and over 30.
To be happily married counts for 0 points.
If your spouse dies that counts for 100 points.
63 for going to jail. 73 for divorce.
Divorce is more stressful than imprisonment.
Getting married is 3 points more stressful
than being fired. Marital reconciliation (45 points)
and retirement (also 45 points)
are only half as stressful as
the death of your spouse.
Minor violations of the law: 11 points.
Trouble with the boss: 23. Christmas: 12. But
sexual difficulties are less stressful
than pregnancy (40 points versus 39).
A mortgage over $10,000 is worse
than a son (or daughter) leaving home.
Trouble with your in-laws is as stressful
as "outstanding personal achievement"
which is only slightly more stressful
than if "wife begins or stops work."
Are you very happy and well-adjusted? 0 points.
Very angry, depressed or frustrated? 20 points.
Conclusion: With 25 points or more, "you probably
will feel better if you reduce your stress."

POST-MODERN

(A Mostly Found Poem)

—With thanks to Richard Lederer's *Fractured English*

"Joan of Arc was married to the Biblical Noah."
"The inhabitants of Egypt were called mummies,
  and built pyramids in the shape of triangular cubes."

"The Pyramids are a range of mountains between France
  and Switzerland."

He graded his papers
  and went home to Honey.

"Areas of the dessert are cultivated by irritation."

Honey and the teacher were newlyweds.
Filing her nails, she watched some Joan Crawford movie.
Handed him a joint.

"Get your papers graded?" Applying nail polish,
Honey reached for *Cosmopolitan*,
turned back to the *TV Guide*.

All pink and red she was
and full of self-esteem and bounce,
teacher's fluorescent bride.

"Now or never," Honey said, her eyes twinkling,
"Post-civilization, post-modern, post-Cracker Jack,
early unforeseeable, post paradigm.

"Now you see it, now you don't."

"They lived in the Sarah Dessert and traveled by Camelot."

"In the dessert, the climate is such
    the inhabitants have to live elsewhere."

"Come and get it," Honey called.
"Come and get it."

"In Europe, the enlightenment was a reasonable time."

Half A Life's History

1983

SCARF GOBBLE WALLOW INVENTORY

How hungry and for what are the people this season
       predicting the end of the end of the end of
I've only just come home after having been away
The world sends its greetings and the greetings
       send greetings
Hello goodbye, hello goodbye
There are greetings and gifts everywhere
Children screaming and feeling slighted
The next minute we're walking along canals
       on the planet Mars
Twenty minutes later we are earthworms in black
       leather jackets, our pockets filled
       with hamburgers,
Voyage to the moon.
All I am really hungry for is everything
The ability to hibernate and a red suitcase going off
       everywhere
Every cell in your body and every cell in my body is
       hungry and each has its own stomach
Are your cells eating my cells? Whose cell is the
       universe, and what is it sick with, if anything?
Is the universe a womb or a mouth?
And what is hunger, really?
And is the end of the world to be understood in terms of
       hunger or gifts, or the tops of peoples' heads
       coming off?

The most complex dream I've ever dreamed I dreamed
        in London.
It involved in its entirety taking one bite of an orange.

* * *

        "What do you want to be when you grow up?" she says.
I'm nearly sixty.
I want to be hungry as I am now and a pediatrician.
The truth is I'm 45 and hungrier than I was when I was
        20 and a sailor.
I'm hungry for ice cream made with ice cream and not
        chemicals or artificial spoons.
I've never been so hungry in my life.
I want one more bacon-lettuce-and-tomato
        sandwich,
to make love and kiss everyone I know goodbye.
Tomorrow at half past four we will all four-and-a-half
        billion of us walk slowly into orbit.
If only one can do this breathing normally, and not trip
        on one's breath or have stomach cramps or clammy
        hands or hysterical needs or a coughing fit or the wish
        to trample or stomp someone, but stepping peacefully
There is ALL the time in the world
There is ALL THE TIME IN THE WORLD
There is all the time in the world.

STATEMENT OF POETICS, OR
GOODBYE TO MYSELF

I wrote for myself for people.
                I've changed,
I've changed since I began writing
                    I write for myself. I believe
more than ever in music, in the sound,
                        however gotten, of music
in people's poetry. Rhyme
more than ever. Talk
                people talking, getting that
into one's poetry that
is my poetics. Love
hate lies laughing stealings
self-confession, self-destruction.
No one has to read them. No one
has to publish them.
                    I am more
and more for unpublished poetry.
That is why I have a pseudonym, that
is why I now publish poetry.
To hell with the Business
of Anthologies. To hell with Anthologies.

One way and another I have written angry
for twenty years. Now I want music and
the sounds of people.
I want poems that use the word *heart* and
self-confession and incorrect

grammar and the soils and stains of Neruda
and Lorca and Kabir and Williams and
Whitman and Yeats.

Forty-four years old. Stand on my head
ten minutes daily morning
breakfast, supper.
Writing less and less.
Evaporating into the air
feet first. I won't
ever die. I'll simply
stand on my head
and disappear into the
air just like that.

I don't believe in imagination. The prairies
as a landscape are imagination. England is,
as a landscape, a failure of imagination.
Kenya is imagination, India
is reaching even further
than that. And that is why I will
go to India, which I will in seven
days time. So this
is a time capsule
in case anyone is
interested and in case
I never come back.

Goodbye for
now, goodbye
goodbye goodbye
to myself,
goodbye goodbye
for now
goodbye myself,
goodbye for
now goodbye.

Poet Santa Cruz

1985

ODE TO SANTA CRUZ

—For sandy Lydon

You want a sunrise? asks the poet,
I'll give you a sunrise. Eggplant cirrus clouds,
pinky smoky blue and gray,
pink, moss pink, pink nether flower
sunrise, sunrise
yellow white silicon chip
foghorn, windchime, no-color haze.

Sunrise sunrise
O City of Mystical Arts and Live Soup,
Antique bathhouse, casino
Riva Fish House,

A busload of German tourists
applauding *(applaudieren!)*
the sunrise.
clam chowder, O scrubbed blue light
melon balls and watermelon shooters,
arcade, pink neon, roller coaster heart-shaped mirror.

KA-BOOM! House begins to dance,
land moves in waves three and four feet high,
weight machines swaying, mirrors rattling,
a sidewalk of broken glass,
a street filled with jewels.

Loma Prieta, The Earthquake of the Dark Hill,
place, this place, always coming back from a disaster.
Natural beauty and unnatural events,
jazz, blues, canoes, tattoos,
I bow and give thanks to the muse,

Santa Cruz, O Santa Cruz!

CASTROVILLE, CALIFORNIA—A SONNET

O thistle-like artichoke in the place
of glory. Green peppers: four lushly framed nudes
staring down on us with a kind of greasy grace.
Purple and green eggplants like immodest prudes.

And apples of heroic size, left to right
like paintings of smugly pompous ancestors.
Broccoli plus pale mushrooms in the moonlight,
whitely bulbous omniscient lecturers

On the care and curatorship of fruit
and vegetables, which play more a part
in our lives than the sad-eyed, ruling dupes
who clutter up our walls displacing fruits.

I never did before, but now I will:
I sing, dear friends, of brave plain Castroville.

Four Incarnations

1991

FOUR INCARNATIONS

Foreword:

Born on the Jewish North Side of Chicago, *bar mitzvahed*, sailor, amnesiac, university professor (Cornell, Iowa, Connecticut College), newspaper editor, food reviewer, father of five children, husband to four wives, my writing career has been described by critic Virginia Lee as a "long and winding road."

1. Switchblade Poetry: Chicago Style

I began writing poetry in Chicago at age 15, when I was named corresponding secretary for a gang of young punks and hoodlums called the Semcoes. A Social Athletic Club, we met at various locations two Thursdays a month. My job was to write postcards to inform my brother thugs—who carried switchblade knives and stole cars for fun and profit—as to when, where and why we were meeting.

Rhyming couplets seemed the appropriate form to notify characters like light-fingered Foxman, cross-eyed Harris, and Irving "Koko," of upcoming meetings. My switchblade juvenilia:

> The Semcoes meet next Thursday night
> at Speedway
> Koko's. Five bucks dues, Foxman, or fight.

Koko was a young boxer whose father owned Chicago's
Speedway Wrecking Company, and whose basement
was filled with punching bags and pinball machines.
Koko and the others joked about my affliction—the
writing of poetry—but were so astonished that they
criticized me mainly for my inability to spell.

2. Sailor Librarian: San Diego

At 17, I graduated from high school, gave up my job
as soda jerk and joined the Navy. The Korean War
was underway; my mother had died, and Chicago seemed
an oppressive place to be.

My thanks to the U.S. Navy. They taught me how
to type (60 words a minute), organize an office, and
serve as a librarian. In 1952 I served in Korea aboard a
300-foot long, flat-bottomed Landing Ship Tank (LST).
A Yeoman 3rd Class, I became overseer of 1200
paperback books, a sturdy upright typewriter, and a
couple of filing cabinets.

The best thing about duty on an LST is the ship's
speed: 8-10 knots. It takes approximately one month
for an LST to sail between San Diego and Pusan, Korea.
In that month I read Melville's *Moby Dick*,
Whitman's *Leaves of Grass*, Thoreau's *Walden*,

Isak Dinesen's *Winter's Tales*, the King James Version
of the Bible, Shakespeare's *Hamlet, King Lear,* and a
biography of Abraham Lincoln.

While at sea, I began writing poetry as if poems,
to paraphrase Thoreau, were secret letters from
some distant land.

I sent one poem to a girl named Lorelei with whom
I was in love. Lorelei had a job at the Dairy Queen.
Shortly before enlisting in the Navy, I spent $15 of
my soda jerk money taking her up in a single engine,
sight-seeing airplane so we could kiss and—at the
same time—get a good look at Chicago from the air.
Beautiful Loreli never responded to my poem. Years
later, at the University of Iowa Writers' Workshop,
I learned that much of what I had been writing (love
poems inspired by a combination of lust and
loneliness) belonged, loosely speaking, to a
tradition—the venerable tradition of unrequited love.

3. Mr. Amnesia: Cambridge

In 1962, after ten years of writing poetry, my book,
Uncle Dog & Other Poems, was published by Putnam
in England. That was followed by two books from
Cornell University Press, *Kissing the Dancer* and

Thousand-Year-Old Fiancée. Then in 1966, I was
invited to do 14 poetry readings in a two-week
stretch at places like Dartmouth, Amherst, and the
University of Connecticut.

The day before I was scheduled to embark on the
reading series, I was hit by a speeding MG in
Cambridge, Massachusetts.

I lost my memory for a period of about 24 hours.
Just as I saw the world fresh while cruising to a
war zone, so I now caught a glimpse of what a city
like Cambridge can look like when one's inner slate,
so to speak, is wiped clean.

4. Santa Claus: Santa Cruz

In December, 1985, recently returned to the U.S.
after some years in Canada, a free lance writer
in search of a story, I sought and found
employment as a Rent-a-Santa Claus. Imagine walking
into the local Community Center and suddenly, at the
sight of 400 children, feeling transformed from
one's skinny, sad-eyed self, into an elf—having to
chant the prescribed syllables, "Ho, Ho, Ho."

What is poetry? For me, it's the restrained music
of a switchblade knife. It's an amphibious warship
magically transformed into a basketball court, and
then transformed again into a movie theater showing
a film about the life of Joan of Arc. It is the
vision of an amnesiac, bleeding from a head injury,
witnessing the play of sunlight on a redbrick wall.

Poetry comes to a bearded Jewish wanderer, pulling
on a pair of high rubber boots with white fur, and a
set of musical sleigh bells, over blue, fleece-lined
sweat pants. It comes to the father of five
children bearing gifts for 400 and, choked up,
unable to speak, alternately laughing and sobbing
the three traditional syllables—Ho, Ho, Ho—hearing
at the same time, in his heart, the more plaintive,
tragic—*Oi vay, Oi vay, Oi vay.*

CLANCY THE DOG

—For Claire

He is so ugly he is a psalm to ugliness,
this extra-terrestrial, short-haired
midget sea lion,
snorts, farts, grunts, turns somersaults
on his mistress' bed.

She calls him an imperfect Boston terrier,
part gnome, part elf,
half something and half something else,
180,000,000-year-old Clancy
with his yellowy-white, pin-pointy teeth
and red, misshapen pre-historic gums.

Clancy has no tail at all and doesn't bark.
He squeaks like a monkey,
flies through the air,
lands at six every morning
on his mistress' head,
begging to be fed and wrapped not in a robe
but a spread.

Tree frog, wart hog, ground hog,
"Clancy, Clancy," she calls for him
in the early morning fog,
and he appears, anything, anything,
part anything, but a dog.

SCARLET THE PARROT

Scarlet perches on the office windowsill
shrieking, hollering, barking

Like a dog. She knocks her mottled beak
against the warehouse window

And tries to open
the metal hook and eye latch.

There are parrot droppings
on the telephone and Scarlet has eaten

Part of the plastic receiver.
The parrot slides like a red fireman

With yellow and blue feathers
up and down the cord,
             holding on

With her beak, maneuvering gracefully
             with her claws.
When I approach she calls, "Hello, hello . . ."

Walks up my trouser leg holding on
with her macaw's beak. I feed the bird

Oranges and pears, almonds
and sunflower seeds.

I swivel my head round and round
in imitation of her neck movements.

"What's happening?" she asks,
and again, "What's happening?"

"Hello, cookie. Yoo-hoo . . .
Can you talk, can you talk?" she asks

Chewing for several minutes,
finally swallowing
            a leather button

Off my green corduroy jacket, threatening,
ready to tear my ear off,

Biting if I place my finger
in her mouth. Her tongue is black

And her beady eyes piercing like an eagle's.
She wants a response, tests my reactions.

Tenderly the parrot walks up my corduroy jacket,
sensually restraining her claws. I'm aroused.

When a dog barks, she barks too: *Rrf, rrf.*
Casually, a relaxed but authentic

Imitation. "Hello, darling," she breathes,
looking me in the eye knowing I know

If it pleases her she might bite my ear off.
"Yoo-hoo, yoo-hoo, now you say something," she says.

ALFA THE DOG

It isn't enough that when I go off for three weeks to an
artists' colony and phone home, the first thing my wife
tells me is there's a new addition to the family, a seven-
month-old poodle named Alfa and that Alfa has papers,
an honest-to-God pedigree that includes not only aristo-
cratic ancestors, but recent appearances in "The New York
Review of Books" and a novel published by Houghton-
Mifflin. And when I am somewhat less than ecstatic,
my wife asks me to at least say a few words to the new
addition, and puts on Alfa the dog. "Speak, Alfa, speak,"
I hear her say. And Alfa who is, by all accounts, loyal
and obedient, a noted storyteller, intelligent and amusing
as Oscar Wilde, refuses to speak, to bark, or make some
witty remark like, "What's the weather like in Saratoga?"
All I hear is Alfa's low doggy breathing and the tinkle
of the elegant silver bell on her collar.

My wife comes back on and says, "I have an idea. You
bark into the phone. Alfa will answer back."

Well, it's only costing a dollar ninety-five a minute and
good-natured soul that I am, devoted to my wife, guilty
at running off for three weeks, I put myself into it, throw
back my head and howl, barking, yowling, yipping like a
real dog—a dog without papers, a dog with fleas, a dog
like one of those mutts I knew growing up in Chicago,
and this happening, of course, on the public pay phone
at Yaddo, the "artists' heaven," what the *New York Times*
calls the Harvard of Artists' Colonies.

Looking up, sure enough, I see one of America's more distinguished composers with his mouth open, his pipe falling to the floor, waiting in line, no doubt, to speak to his wife and children and his cats and dogs.

"Well, darling," I say, "we've been talking for twenty-five minutes. This is going to cost a fortune."

At that moment, Alfa decides she wants to make her presence known to all concerned, and she begins barking into the phone, answering me in kind, responding yip for yip, and yap for yap, lest there be any doubt in anyone's mind as to who it is I have been speaking— me to Alfa the dog, Alfa the dog to me.

BASKETBALL'S THE AMERICAN GAME
BECAUSE IT'S HYSTERICAL

"Basketball's the American game because it's hysterical,"
says Lorrie Goldensohn as the players and coaches come
off the bench and the crowd is on its feet yelling and
the Knicks are ahead 97-95 with just over three minutes
to go in the fourth quarter and Perry hits from the side
and Lorrie's husband, Barry, comes downstairs with a
bottle of scotch and a guide to English verse.

"Unless there is
a new mind, there cannot be a new line," he reads
refilling our glasses.
"Without invention the line
will never again take on its ancient
divisions . . ."

All evening we have been watching the New York Knicks
battling the Boston Celtics and having a running
argument about free verse, traditional rhyming poetry,
syllabic verse ("what's the point in counting for
counting's sake?"), the critic Hugh Kenner, John
Hollander's *Rhyme's Reason*, the variable foot and
the American idiom.

"In and out by Williams," says the announcer, "he's got
a nose for the basket." The crowd is on its feet
again, roaring.

"We know nothing and can know nothing
but the dance, to dance to a measure
                contrapuntally,
Satyrically, the tragic foot," Barry continues.

The Celtics race down the court. "Talk about the
green wave coming at you." Bird hits and the Celtics
even the score.

"Basketball's the American game because it's like the
variable foot," says Lorrie, "it's up in the air
all the time. It's quick and the floor is continually
moving and there's this short back and forth factor."

"What I like best about the game," I say, "is shutting
my eyes and tuning out the announcer and hearing
Barry read and arguing about poetry and drinking
and listening all the while to the music of
seven-foot black herons in gym shoes, ten giant
gazelles, the stirring squeak of twenty over-size
sneakers on the varnished floor, a floor which
has been carefully and ingeniously miked in advance
for sound."

ON MY WAY TO THE KOREAN WAR

—For President Dwight Eisenhower

On my way to the Korean War,
I never got there.
One summer afternoon in 1952,
I stood instead in the bow
of the Attack Transport *Menard*,
with an invading force
of 2,000 battle-ready Marines,
watching the sun go down.
Whales and porpoises,
flying fish and things jumping
out of the water.
Phosphoresence—
Honolulu behind us,
Inchon, Korea, and the war ahead.

Crew cut, 18-year-old librarian,
Yeoman 3rd Class, editor
of the ship's newspaper,
I wrote critically if unoriginally
of our Commander-in-Chief,
Mr. President,
and how perplexing it was that he
would launch a nuclear-powered submarine
while invoking the Lord,
Crocodile Earth shaker,
Shiva J. Thunderclap,
choosing the occasion to sing
the now famous *Song of the Armaments,*
the one with the line *"weapons for peace"*:

        O weapons for peace,
        O weapons for peace,
        awh want, awh want
        more weapons for peace!

At sundown, a half dozen sailors
converged on the bow of the ship
where, composed and silent,
we'd maintain our vigil
until the sun had set.

Careful to avoid being conspicuous,
no flapping or flailing of the arms,
no running, horizontal take-offs,
one man, then another, stepped out into space,
headed across the water,
moving along as if on threads.
After a while, I did the same:
left my body just as they left theirs.

        In-breathe, out-breathe, and leave,
        in-breathe, out-breathe, and leave.
        Leave your body, leave your body,
        leave your body, leave your body,

we sang as we went out
to where the light went,
and whatever held us to that ship
and its 2,000 battle-ready troops, let go.
So it was, dear friends, I learned to fly.
And so in time must you
and so will the warships,
and the earth itself,
and the sky,
for as the prophet says, the day cometh
when there will be no earth left to leave.

      O me, O my,
      O me, O my,
      goodbye earth, goodbye sky.
      Goodbye, goodbye.

1950s / 1960s

Pre-med
thinking he's
got to learn about the world
all over again from
      square one

Doesn't think he knows anything for sure
only the hula-hoops and Twinkies,
the blues and violets of his mind
      very late at night

red and pink lipstick case
with a little mirror on one side,
hat, stockings, garter belt
      and gloves

He bought a shirt in 1950 the most remarkable
      feature of which is
that a snag or tear will reduce it
      to nothing.

It's a shirt made of a single cell
that, when it's reduced to nothing,
a single cell remains.
      The original cell of that fabric.

What he is seeking is a quilt
made up of the original cells of all the fabrics.

What the 1950s does
like a blow to the back or side of one's head
it relocates your mind

                    * * *

'Delicious' apples and the popularity of DDT

James Dean
Peter Lawford,
Elizabeth Taylor,
            the Mickey Mouse Club
                    taken seriously

The time many people who came into their own
            in the 1960s
first got laid

The Rosenberg's frying in the electric chair
            McCarthy and his crony Roy Cohn
the atomic bomb already five years old

Nixon: "California politics is a can of worms"
Captain Kangaroo, Howdy Doody

                    * * *

Inhaling
The jazz was good
Death was softened, advancements made
in the salesmanship of everything

His own deepest impulses
            were not to nurse or nurture
            but to hang out again
at Sonny Berkowitz' Pool Hall,
wearing blue suede shoes,
Levis and navy blue shirt.
He bought a zip gun,
joined a street gang

Once, joint in hand,
exploring the intricacies
of the Chicago Drainage Canal,
he entered a sewer
and ambled deeply as he could
reflecting all the while
on his chances of surviving
the synchronized flushing
of three-and-a-half million toilets.

For the first time in 2,000 years
one went four years to a University
without hearing one true word;
going to work for Hallmark Greeting cards

or the phone company
one knew something was at hand because things
became easy.
Tin-Pan alley
people in college dormitories subscribing
          to Photoplay
and *The Nail Polish Review.*

Five foot two, eyes of blue,
cotton candy hair
fluffy lavender
          angora sweater
short white socks
with fat cuffs
one of a hundred couples
in a Champaign, Illinois
dormitory lounge.

Rock Hudson singing to Doris Day,
"... beautiful girl,
your eyes, your hair
is beyond compare ..."
(Pillow Talk)

"Touch me, touch me,"
guiding his hand
into her pleated wool skirt,
'petting' it was called,

one foot touching the floor at all times
ejaculating
somewhere or other
somehow or other
discreetly as possible
love in the 1950s.

He sees giant mushroom cloud
father of the H-Bomb Edward Teller

an entire island,
Eniwetok,
radioactive coral dust
                a gigantic cauliflower, blue and gray
and mauve . . .
five million tons of TNT

Police Action Korea Harry Truman
and Dwight David Eisenhower,
each with six legs and arms
dancing to the music
        of Lord Shiva and Judy Garland
        doing it
                on a pink velvet loveseat

some twenty-five miles into the stratosphere,
and spread a hundred miles across the sky.

ODE TO TORPOR

Glory be to God for the tiresome and tedious,
Glory be to God for tedium,
for no news about anything,

for newspaper strikes and power outages,
lethargy and downtime.

Postpone and delay. And again,
                              postpone and delay.
No place to go. No way to get there.
No reason not to stay.

Glory be to God for inaction,
for not getting things done,
for not getting anything done,

No huffin', no puffin',
just some of that slow and easy,
the woman lackadaisically on top,
the man lackadaisically on top.
Yummy, yummy, take your time,
yummy, yummy, I'll take mine.

Slow and easy,
slow and easy.
Glory be to God, O glory.

O glory be to God.

SAUSALITO FERRY POEM

"Okay, we're here! Stop scribbling,"
she shouts back at me
climbing down the iron ladder
expecting me to follow.

The boat goes sailing off
to Tiburon,
me with one-half a new poem standing
waving at her from the railing.

"Pink light round your white body,
your blue eyes flashing," I sing
into the wind.
"What's that you're saying? I forgot
to get off?
It's all over now between us?

"All I care about is poetry?
O listen, my love, just listen.
You know that's not true.
I know you'll like this one,
these lines
written exclusively for you."

FOR GLORIA ON HER 60TH BIRTHDAY, OR LOOKING FOR LOVE IN MERRIAM-WEBSTER

"Beautiful, splendid, magnificent,
delightful, charming, appealing,"
        says the dictionary.
And that's how I start . . . But I hear her say,
"Make it less glorious and more Gloria."

Imperious, composed, skeptical, serene,
lustrous, irreverent,
she's marked by glory, she attracts glory
"Glory," I say, "Glory, Glory."

"Is there a hallelujah in there?"
she asks, when I read her lines one and two.
"Not yet," I say, looking up from my books.
She protests, "Writing a poem isn't the same

"As really attending to me." "But it's for
your birthday," I say. Pouting,
playfully cross, "That's the price you pay
when your love's a poet."

She has chestnut-colored hair,
old fashioned Clara Bow lips,
moist brown eyes . . .
                arms outstretched, head thrown back
she glides toward me and into her seventh decade.

Her name means "to adore,"
"to rejoice, to be jubilant,
to magnify and honor as in worship, to give or ascribe glory—"
my love, O Gloria, I do, I do.

HANNAH

Her third eye is strawberry jam
has a little iris in it
her eyelids
        are red
she's sleepy
        and the milk
        has gone down
        the wrong way.
I've just had breakfast
with the smallest person in the world.

PORTRAIT OF AN L.A. DAUGHTER

Take #1

Braided blonde hair
white and pink barrettes
Bette Davis gorgeous
I hug her
dreamy daughter with no make-up
silver skull and crossbones
middle
        finger
              ring
three or four others in each ear
rings in her navel
rings on her thumbs
gentle moonchild
        "pal" she announces
to "Porno for Pyros"
formerly the group "Jane's Addiction"
"Nothing's Shocking"
with Perry Farrell
Dave Navarro on guitar
and Stephen Perkins
on drums
Ain't No Right they sing.
"What are you,
        some kind of groupie?" I ask.
She says nothing.
        Just turns up the volume.

Been Caught Stealing
          they sing.

I hold her
Wet 'n' Wild lip gloss
diamond stud earrings
and glitter on her cheeks

Wan, she's looking wan
my dancing daughter

Hannah Davi–a new name–
walk-on in the movie *Day of Atonement*
          with Christopher Walken

And a part in a Levitz Furniture ad
          ("it's work")
and a part in an MCI commercial
          ("Best Friends")
breaking in
Brotherhood Of Justice

a Swiss Alps bar-maid
("classic blonde Gretel")
in a Folger's Coffee commercial

"Grunge is in," she says
visiting Santa Cruz,
"any Goodwill's around?"

* * *

Flashback

Appearing,
      "crowning" says the doctor

"Hannah" says her mother
"the name means 'grace'"

Two-year-old drooling
as I toss her into space
and back
      she falls
and back
into space again

Flawless teeth and perfect smile
one blue eye slightly larger than the other
her three-thousand miles away mother
still present as
two as one
two breathing together
we three breathe again as one
Hannah O Hannah

WATER BREATHER

1. SWIMMER IN AIR

Gulper of sea,
swimmer in air,

he dives, dives in again
again
      water's
           water,
air is air.

"Water's
           water,
air is air,"
      I say.
"No," he says, "no."

He's the breather of water,
three-year-old refuser,
          won't be taught.

Intent, he makes his run,
big feet slapping, loopy leap
and sinks
     to the bottom.

Swim to him.

"Water's

                water," I begin . . .
he's red-eyed, sputtering, shaking—
Clambers up the ladder

                    to the dock
              and jumps.

Scoop and hug him close
              hold him out.

"Stroke, stroke
           inhale

                  in air
exhale in water," I say,
      "like this, Michael."
"Breathe in air,

             swim in water."

"No," he says, "no."

      Slap, slap, his feet
on the side of the dock

He breathes in water
and swims in the air

breathes in water
and swims in air.

2. JULY 4

A boy achieves maximum pissing power at age 5 or 6....
—Dr. Ed Jackson

"Michael, what the—"

six-year-old, dick in hand,
turning, his stream unbroken,

nine feet if it's an inch,
          laughing, the kid's laughing
as he circles

360-degrees
hand all the time on the throttle,
slowly, back arched

he stands
          "Dick, dink, decker,
              weener, peter, pecker . . ." he sings
crowd gathering

nine feet from VW rooftop
to raging Mr. Beer-In-His-Hand.
"Is that your kid up there?"

I should laugh,
      get up there with him,
lead our friends in applause.

     "Dick, dink, decker," he sings,
face shining, joy to the world.

Rein him in, *do something,*
Jesus K. Christ,

"Dance," I want to say, "dance
on the roof of the German machine.

"Piss on, piss all you want—
What a stream!" I want to say.

Old fool, old scold,
too fearful to sing
"O Stream of Gold . . ."

Fucked father, fucked-up father,
I spank him instead.

3. HOUSE BOAT

Lasqueti Island, B.C.

Washing dishes in the darkness
with a hose,
I spray off the few
      remnants
of spaghetti onto the oysters

In their beds below.
Inside the single room
there is no running water—
      only the green hose
on the deck of our floating home.

We secure the lines,
bathe and sing, *We all live in a Yellow Submarine* . . .
I reach out in the darkness
hearing my son brushing his teeth
to borrow his toothbrush.

I cannot find my own:
Tasting
      my fourteen-year-old son's
mouth inside my mouth.
Then we find more dishes

And, as the moon rises and the lines
        go tight,
continue scrubbing and drying silverware
and plates,
        two dishwashers reading Braille.

4. MOUNTAIN SOLITAIRE

Jerome, Arizona

He's thirty-two, my age
when he was born.
Haven't seen him for four years,
estranged son of estranged wife.

Phone:
        "Please . . . leave . . . message . . ."
              says the machine.
"Hey, Michael . . . It's Dad!"
He won't pick up, won't call back.

I court him, send gifts:
        "Oh, boy, a cordless phone
from, let's see now, Mr. Walk-around . . .
my much-doodling daddy!"

I see him shake his head.
And write, I write him a poem.
Read it onto his answering machine.
      "Dick, dink, decker,
          weener, peter, pecker . . ."

He's away—a girlfriend
 plays back the message.
"There's a stalker . . ." she tells him.
"No, that's my father," he says,
 and calls me. He likes the poem.

                * * *

—*Golden Gate Park*

We meet and he leads me
to the Hall of Flowers,
his dark hair combed forward,
bushing out over his ears,
      single white strand glinting in the sun.

He's three, six and thirty-two;
I'm thirty-two, thirty-eight and sixty-four.
The prodigal father
      and the abandoned 'live alone,'
Mr. Mountain Solitaire.

We stroll through the Garden of Fragrance,
oasis of lakes.

                                 Absentee father

fathering,

he the fathered, fatherless
hungering

            son to be a father
            father to be father

This is the hunger.

FASHION MAKES THE HEART GROW FONDER

Marriage and hanging go by destiny.
—Robert Burton, *Anatomy of Melancholy*

Partygoers
Her fruity, floral fragrance—
Honey at her dressing table
          like a pilot in the cockpit,
a woman armed with old *TV Guides*, catalogs,
ordering information
          for all the major scents and potions.

She put on (how can I describe them?)
refrigerator avocado green
          and white
Keith Partridge bell-bottoms. Incandescent,
no less bizarre, I wore purple velveteen pants
and a tie-dyed shirt.

Her old lover Warren was there in his pimp suit,
          giant bug-eye sunglasses
and huge fake fur pimp hat,
a party with vintage Joan Crawford movies,
Honey wearing Chanel Number 5,
          the first synthetic scent.

And me, her consort, I wore
'a blend of crisp citrus and warm spice, mossy woods, a scent
for the feeling man.'

I remember her silver and turquoise earrings
on the make-up table

as the bed jumped and jerked
those first two years.

Ravi Shankar, Thai weed, and a little homegrown,
that velvet ribbon choker with butterflies
and the scent of Honey when she dropped her
            tooled leather belt on the floor.

Then, "Tell me what you want," I said.
"You can't give me what I want."
"What do you want?"
"I'm out of style and so are you.
 I want to lose weight."

And like that it was over.

"How about this handbag?" offered *Cosmo*,
"the perfect accessory
 to the outfit you wear
 when you leave your husband."

And that's how it ended. Honey at some fashion show
throwing back her head, the spotlight playing
on her face and neck.

Yes, I could see what Honey wanted,
to shop where she'd never shopped before,
to pull on high leather boots

and a mini-skirt; then, beaded Navaho handbag in hand,
flashing a little scented thigh, walking out on someone
who couldn't keep up,
a jerk in tie-dye.

I loved the woman, longed to stay with her and,
to do so, if I could have, arm-in-arm with her,
I'd have walked out on myself.

MY MUSE

As a rule, the power of absolutely falling in love soon vanishes . . . because the woman feels
embarrassed by the spell she exercises over her poet-lover and repudiates it . . .
—Robert Graves, *The White Goddess*

"Why don't you just write a poem, right now?" she says.
'Western wind, when wilt thou blow . . .'
why don't you write a poem like that,
like that 'Anonymous'? Something inspirational."

"Talk about muses," I sulk,
"Yeats' wife was visited in her dreams by angels
saying, 'We have come to bring you images
for your husband's poetry.'"

"Yeah? So what?" she says. "It's out of style.
I already do too much for you."

Odalisque in a wicker chair,
book open on her lap,
dry Chardonnay at her side,
hand on a dozing, whiskered Sphinx.

"You need a muse," she says, "someone beautiful, mysterious,
some long-lost love,
            fragile, a dancer perhaps. Look at me . . ."

"Yeah?" I say, refilling her glass,
"You hear me complaining? You're *zaftig*."
            "Zaftig?"
"Firm, earthy, juicy, too," I say.

* * *

"Juicy plum," I say, in bed, left hand over her head,
"rose petals," I say, right arm around her.
"Silver drop earrings," I murmur, ordering out
for gifts. "Aubergine scarf, gray cashmere cardigan."

I do this in my sleep. Go shopping in my sleep.
"Oh, yeah, and a case of Chardonnay."
Wake to the scent of apple blossoms,
decades in the glow of rose light.

* * *

"Wake," she whispers. I tell her my dream.
We kiss. Poppy Express. Racy Red. Red Coral.
            Star Red.
                    Red red.

"Enough. That's enough," she says.

ONE FOR THE ROAD

One for the road.
A little detached it was, but bouncy, flouncy, hoochie coochie,
woo wah woo, out there under the stars,
woo wah woo,
one for the road, one for the road it was,
and end of the show.
Stupid shit, how was I to know?
One for the road and end of the show?
So good-humored it was, I missed the clue,
hugging and kissing, all that
hugging and kissing.
Missed just how all over it really was.

TURNING 60

The first 40 years of life give us the text; the next 30 supply the commentary on it . . .
—Schopenhauer

1. *Homework*

According to Webster, the word six derives from the Latin
"sex" [s-e-x] and the Greek "hex" [h-e-x].
Six units or members
as, an ice-hockey team;
a 6-cylinder engine;
six fold, six-pack, sixpenny nail, six-
shooter, sixth sense.

"Zero" denotes the absence of all magnitude, the point of departure
in reckoning; the point from which the graduation of a scale
(as of a thermometer) begins;
zero hour,
zeroth,
as, "the zero power of a number."

Zero, the great "there's nothing there" number,
a blast off into a new decade.

2. *Grammar as Hymnal*

Seeking solace in a review of grammar, I turned to Strunk & White's
Elements of Style. Standing at attention,
opening to the section on usage, I chanted and sang—
uniting my voice with the voices of others, the vast chorus
of the lovers of English.

We sing of verb tense, past, present and future.
We sing the harmony of simple tenses.
We lift our voice in praise of action words,
   and the function of verb tense.

We sing of grammar which is our compass
providing, as it does, clues as to how
we might navigate the future,
at the same time it
illuminates the past.

As a teacher, I talk. That's present.
For thirty years as a teacher, I talked. That's past.
It may only be part time, but I will talk. That's future.

3. *Living the Future Perfect*

I will have invoked the muse.

I will have remembered to give thanks, knowing our origins
are in the invisible, and that we once possessed boundless energy,
but were formless, and that we are here to know
'the things of the heart through touching.'

I will have remembered, too, that there is only one thing we all possess equally and that is our loneliness.

I will have loved.
You will have loved.
We will have loved.

God Is In the Cracks

2006

SON OF THE COMMANDMENT

Chicago

"So, twelve years old! Soon you'll be *bar mitzvah*,
         a *mensch*, a human being. Yes, son,
a human being, you. 'Today I am a man,' you'll say,
like I did. Let's see what you know:
The serpent in the Bible, what language does he speak?

"What's wrong with you? He speaks Hebrew. Same as God.
Same as Abraham and Isaac.
Same as Jesus.
Who else speaks Hebrew?

"Adam and Eve. Noah, too, and the animals:
 the giraffe, the kangaroo, the lion.
         Hebrew.
                Hebrew.
 Soon you'll speak Hebrew.
 Yes, and you'll read it too. *Apostate!*

"You're going to Hebrew School.

"Why? So you can speak to God in His own language.
 Lesson One: *Bar* means son, *mitzvah* means commandment.
 Bar mitzvah: Son of the commandment.
 Commandment, *mitzvah*: What God gave to Moses.

"Lesson Two: When did Jews get souls?

"Souls they got when they got *Torah*.
Torah. *Torah* is Commandments.
Torah is soul.

"So learn, *bar mitzvah* boy! Read. Learn the blessing.
 Do it right and you'll see
                    the letters fly up to heaven.

"Learn. Yes. There's money
                    in puberty,
                 money in learning. Books, money, fountain
pens . . . Always remember: learning is the best merchandise.

"Lesson Three: *Daven* means pray. You rock back and forth
                 like the rabbi,
                          and pray. In Hebrew.
From your mouth to God's ear.
But it has to be in Hebrew.
And you can't mispronounce:
And no vowels to make it easy."

A PRAYER FOR MY MOTHER

May the Great Name be blessed . . .

1. Mother's Limousines

"Mourn like a Jew," Grandfather Max says,
  tearing my shirt
                from the collar down,
"and when she's buried, rip out the grass
          and wail.
Expose your heart. Lament for her."

> *Mother, mother*
> *mother of the inflamed heart.*

Car door slamming behind us as we exit . . .

Bar-mitzvah'd boy, 14, I say it once,
say what I'm told to say,
"He is the Rock, His work is perfect . . ."
Say it,
            YIT-GA-DAL
            V'YIT-KA-DASH
            SH'MEI
            RA-BA
            B'AL MA . . .
        the Kaddish of sounds, not words

"May a great peace from heaven . . ." I say,
"May His great Name be blessed,
  . . . Magnified and sanctified . . .

Y'HAY
SH'LAMA
RA-BA
MIN SH'MAYA
V'CHAYIM
    ALENU . . . I say.

. . . a week later,
        no to the rabbi,
        no to morning,
        no to twilight,
            no to the mid-day prayer
no repeating the prayer three times a day for a year
        no, I say, and no to the *shul.*

        "We're animals first and human second," she says, "and there is no God.
        Do you hear me?"

Fox-trotting mother. Dancer mother. Beauty Queen
        in the house of prayer.

            "Mom," I ask, "how do you pray?"
            She shakes her head and turns away.
                "Snap out of it," she says.

            "Better to go shopping," she says,
            "better to get a job, better to make money."
            I reach out. "Mom—"

"Hands off," she says, "hands off."

"Kids," she says. "*Oi vay.*"
"Holocaust," she says. "*Oi, oi, oi.*"
"God," she says. "What God?"

"Bless the Lord who is blessed," I don't pray.
"May the Great Name be blessed," I don't pray,
        but burn a candle so Mother,
 Miss Chicago,
                can find her way back.

                Later, I cannot recall her face.
                ". . . you're not to look on any photo of her,
                        not for seven days," says Grandfather.
                What did she even look like?
                Faceless son
                        mourning a faceless mother,
                        mourning her,
                mourning
                        freelance,
                mourning on the fly.

"She'll wander for seven days," Grandfather says,
"then, when she's wormed, her soul will return to God."

                lacks a body and I can't recall her face
                lacks a body and I can't recall her face

"Save her soul from *Gehenna*.
Join us," pleads the rabbi.
                    No, no is my prayer
No to duty and no to prayer.

Who was she? Some brunette rich girl
I never knew,
            a stranger dead at 42.
Mother, the beautiful secretary.
I touch her in a dream. She turns,
and there's no one there.

I shake from head to foot.
I stand and I sway.
"Mother, Mother," I say.

Blessed be the stranger.
No, no to the stranger,
no to the stranger.

No is my Kaddish.
No is my prayer.
I am the no
I am the not.

I will not be her savior,
I will not.

2. Gehenna, or Purgatory

                Mother applies Pond's Beauty Cream. Her face glistens.
                Massages her forehead with one hand,
                holds the other to her heart.

               "What's the point?" she asks, cigarette ablaze,
                       mouth tightening.

When she dies, they bury her not in a shroud, but in pancake make-up
                  and best gray dress.

"Turn the photos to the wall," says Grandfather,
"and cover your lips.
                    That's right. Now cover your face.
Isolate yourself—groan—let your hair grow wild.
The mourner is the one without a skin, says the Talmud.
Understand? You are no longer whole."
And I think: *I am going to die, too.*

Sit in silence and say nothing.

               "How about a prayer to locusts?" I pray,
               "How about a prayer to boils?

               "O murdering heaven," I pray.

Grandfather cooks lentils,
lentils and eggs. "Mourners' food," he calls it.

"A prayer to rats,
                    and a prayer to roaches."

"Death is the mother of beauty," he says.
"The death of another makes you want to die," he says.
"The Angel of Death is made entirely of eyes," Grandfather says.

                    Damn seeing,
                    Damn touching.
                    Damn feeling.
                    Damn loving.

In Jewish hell—

                    I am the unknowing,
                    the not Jewish Jew.

Split, cloven,
            cracked

                    In hell

                    nameless,
                    and eyeless,
                                faceless.
                    No, no to blessings,
                    no to teachings,
                    no to reading from right to left.

                    I pray with them,

I pray with the no, I pray with the not.
I pray with the dead, I pray with the damned.

God, God who is a wound, we pray.

3. Against Darkness

"Kaddish is a song against darkness," says the rabbi.
YIT-GA-DAL
V'YIT-KA-DASH
SH'MEI
RA-BA
B'AL MA . . .

        "'Magnified and sanctified
        May His Great Name Be . . .'
No it says, no to darkness. No to nothingness.
        'May His Great Name be blessed.'
Kaddish praises God . . .
Kaddish: a mourner's prayer
that never mentions death.
Y'HAY
SH'LAMA
RA-BA
MIN SH'MAYA
V'CHAYIM . . .

"Now then, Let R__, the son of G__,
      come forward," says the rabbi,

but I freeze, pretend not to hear.
Again he calls, calls me to say Kaddish.
(Loudly) "Let R__, son of G__, step beside me."
Ten other mourners turn in my direction.

Again I pretend not to hear.
Staring, face crimson, then white, he turns
       and continues with the service.

                 The Lord is our God, the Lord is One . . .
                 I mourn her—mourn Kaddish—mourn *shul*
                 and head for home. Age 14, I walk out
                         looking
           for stones
               I might hurl into heaven.

                       * * *

I am the un-*bar'd mitzvah,*
escaped
       Jew from nowhere,
apostate,
skipped Jew,
       cleft Jew,
Jew, pause in the beating of the heart.

                       * * *

Once home, I pray, "Damn Him,
    "damn G-d," I pray.

* * *

Mother, car door slamming,
        the shovel biting
Mother, whose body is the world,
        spinning into space—

"Life rattles," she says.
"My son, His Royal Highness," she says,
        "get used to it."

"Mom, is there an afterlife?"
"Shape up," she says. "You are my afterlife.
        God help us."

4. Anniversary

"We're just subdivisions of one person.
One's no better than any other.
Someone dies and you move forward
        into the front lines," Grandfather says,
            lighting a *yortzeit* candle.

                    "'Blessed art thou who raises the dead . . .'"

Shaking the match, he turns. "*Gottenyu!*" he says.

"I should have been next."
Tears well up
         and I see him see her
                          in me.

"Same color hair,
         same eyes . . ." Grandfather says.
"Remember seeing her in her coffin?" he asks,
         grabbing my arm.
"Your mother didn't believe, but she'll be raised
 and rest with G-d. Does love quit?

"Can you feel her . . . hear her inside you?"
 I nod.
"Where?"
"Here, in my chest."
"And what does she say?"

"She says nothing," I reply,
 but she does:
         "Loopy doop," she says, "Rest in peace!
         Wait'll you die, you'll see. There is no peace. When you're dead,
                          you're dead.
                          Enough.
         Meshugge!" she says, and shakes her head.

"Pray, damn you," he says. "It's your mother."

". . . Now it's over," he sobs.
        "But you, the un-mourner
will mourn for her all your life.

"Jew, Jew without beginning," he mocks,
"Jew who got away."

ROSICRUCIAN IN THE BASEMENT

1.

"What's to explain?" he asks.
He's a closet meditator. Rosicrucian in the basement.
In my father's eyes: dream.
"There are two worlds," he says,
    liquid-filled crystal flask

                                and yellow glass egg
on the altar.
He's the "professional man"—
        so she calls him, my stepmother.
That, and "the Doctor":
"The Doctor will see you now," she says,
        working as his receptionist.
He's a podiatrist—foot surgery a specialty—
        on Chicago's North Side.
Russian-born Orthodox Jew
        with *zaftig* Polish wife, posh silvery white starlet
        Hilton Hotel hostess.

2.

This is his secret.
This is where he goes when he's not making money.
The way to the other world is into the basement
and he can't live without this other world.
"If he has to, he has to," my stepmother shrugs.

Keeps door locked when he's not down there.
Keeps the door locked when he is.
"Two nuts in the mini-bar," she mutters, banging pots
            in the kitchen upstairs.
Anyway, she needs to protect the family.
"Jew overboard," she yells, banging dishes.
"Peasant!" he yells back.

3.

"There are two worlds," he says lighting incense, "the seen
    and the unseen, and she doesn't understand.
This is my treasure," he says,
                    lead cooking in an iron pan,
    liquid darkness and some gold.
"Son, there are three souls: one, the Supernal;
            two, the concealed
                            female soul, soul like glue . . .
    holds it all together . . ."
"And the third?" I ask.
We stand there, "I can't recall."
He begins to chant and wave incense.
No *tallis*, no *yarmulke*,
    just knotty pine walls and mini-bar
            size of a ouija board,
    a little schnapps and shot glasses
    on the lower shelf,
    and I'm no help.
Just back from seven thousand dollar trip,

four weeks with Swami Muktananda,
          thinking
Now there's someone who knew how to convert
the soul's longing into gold.
Father, my father: he has this emerald tablet
       with a single word written on it
and an arrow pointing.

* * *

JESUS

"What's with the cross? You believe in Jesus, dad?"
"What?"
"Are you still a Jew?"
 He turns away.
"Dammit, it's not a religion, *farshtehst*?"
      Brings fist down on the altar.
"We seek the perfection of metals," he says,
      re-lighting stove,
          "salvation by smelting."

"But what's the point?" I ask.

"The point? Internal alchemy, *shmegegge*. *Rosa mystica*," he shouts.
Meat into spirit, darkness into light."

Seated now, seated on bar stools.

Flickering candle in a windowless room.
Visible and invisible. Face of my father
        in the other world.
I see him, see him in me
my rosy cross
                podiatrist father.
"I'm making no secret of this secret," he says,
    turning to the altar.
"Tell me, tell me how to pray."
"Burst," he says, "burst like a star."

* * *

ROSY CROSS FATHER

"Yes, he still believes. Imagine—
        American Jews,
                when they die,
roll underground for three days
to reach the Holy Land.
He believes that."

We're standing at the Rosicrucian mini-bar listening,
(clash of pots in the kitchen upstairs)
                father
        with thick, dark-rimmed glasses
blue-denim shirt,
        bristly white mustache,
dome forehead.

"Your stepmother's on the phone with her sister," he says.

"He thinks he can look into the invisible,"
            she says from above.
"He thinks he can peek into the other world,
  like God's out there waiting for him . . .
  Meshugge!"

She starts the dishwasher.

"As above, so below," he says.
"I'm not so sure," I say.
"Listen, everyone's got some stink," he says,
            grabbing my arm,
                        "you think you're immune?"
  I shake my head.

"To look for God is to find Him, " he says.
"If God lived on earth," she says, "people would knock out
            all His windows."
"Kibbitzer," he yells back. "Gottenyu! Shiksa brain!"

  Father turns to his "apparatus,"
"visual scriptures," he calls them,
            tinctures and elixirs,
                        the silvery dark and the silvery white.

"We of the here-and-now, pay our respects
to the invisible.
                    Your soul is a soul," he says, turning to me,
"but body is a soul, too. As the poet says,
'we are the bees of the golden hive of the invisible.'"
"What poet, Dad?"
"The poet! Goddammit, the poet," he yells.

He's paler these days, showing more forehead,
                thinning down.

"We live in darkness and it looks like light.
Now listen to me: I'm unhooking from the world, understand?
Everything is a covering,
contains its opposite.
The demonic is rooted in the divine.
Son, you're an Outside," he says,
            "waiting for an Inside.
but I want you to know . . ."
"Know what, Dad?"
"I'm gonna keep a place for you in the other world."

HEAVENLY SEX

1. The Law

Opens a bottle of schnapps. "Writer, *schmyter*,
you're unemployed.
Unemployed people must make love
at least once a day.
Talmud says:
      A laborer, twice a week; a mule driver
once a week; a camel driver,
once a month. It's the law.
This is heavenly sex. Say a blessing—
pray—'Blessed art thou, O Lord our God . . .'
Ba-ruch a-ta . . .
For your spouse and for your seed.
What is it with you?
I need to explain how to bring a soul into the world?"

2. The Blessing

"Listen:
The soul is the Lord's candle.
So you say a blessing. And you sing to her—your wife:
Strength and honor are her clothing, you sing.
She opened her mouth with wisdom, you sing.
Her children arise up and call her blessed, you sing.
Rabbi says if knowing a woman were not holy,
      it would not be called 'knowing.'
So, after a good *Shabbes* meal—

linen tablecloth, blessed spices,
braided loaves of *challah*,
a goblet of wine . . .
Thirty-nine things you cannot do on the Sabbath,
but you can eat. You can drink. You can *schtupp*.
Make one another happy.
It's the law."

WEDDING #2

1. Temple Parking Lot

Father, removing glasses:
"So, my son is getting married!"

For the second time, dad.

"Yes, but weddings heal. Our Talmud says
a wedding frees bride and groom
        from all past transgressions.
A wedding fixes all that's broken."

You mean one marriage can fix another?

He grabs my arm: "A happy marriage
gives eternal dispensation."

His eyes gather light.
"The Talmud says intercourse is one-sixtieth
the pleasure of paradise."

I'm wearing five-eyelet Florsheims
        with new arch supports.

"This is good." He waves to friends.
"Just don't fumble the goblet."

The goblet?

"The goblet you break after the vows.
This time use your heel. Smash it on the first try.
People'll be watching. Miss it and they'll laugh—
            like last time.
Don't fumble the goblet."

2. Temple Steps

Leads with his chin.
Visible and invisible.
Chin trembling, his face shining.

"I was an orphan."

Yes, I know, dad.

"Did you know an orphan's dead parents
  are able to attend the wedding?"

But dad, I'm not an orphan.

"Well, I just want you to know if you were,
                we'd come anyway.
You know, your grandparents will be there too."

How will they manage that?

"What are you asking? They'll manage.
These are your grandparents:
Grandpa Hyman. Grandmother Bessie.
It's a tradition. Our Talmud says
if they have their bodies, they'll come with their bodies."

But they're dead.

"So, they'll come without."

3. Temple Washroom

"When a man unites with his wife,
God is between them.
I'm telling you: lovemaking is ceremony.
The Talmud says.
You, you're not holy, but your wife is.
With her
        you go to a world outside the world."

So?

"So wash your hands before
        not after.
Wash for the pure and holy bride."
                But what about hygiene?

"How did I bring you up?
Shame on you.
The socks come off and you make love.
The Talmud says. And you make her happy.
Schtupp. Schtupp. Do you understand?
Forget hygiene!
This is the pure and holy bride."

New Poems

Good News From The Other World

ONE-STOP FOOT SHOP

"We walk with angels
and they are our feet."

"'Vibrating energy packets,'" he calls them. "'Bundles of soul
in a world of meat.' Early warning system—
                                    dry skin and brittle nails;
feelings of numbness and cold;
these are symptoms; they mean something.
I see things physicians miss."

"All you have to do is open your eyes, just open your eyes,
and you'll see: seven-eighths of everything is invisible, a spirit
inside the spirit.
The soul is rooted in the foot.
As your friend Bly says, 'The soul longs to go down';
feet know the way to the other world,
that world where people are awake.
So do me a favor: dream me no dreams.
A dreamer is someone who's asleep."

"You know, the material world is infinite,
but boring infinite," he says, cigarette in hand,
little wings fluttering at his ankles.

"And women," he says, smacking his head,
"four times as many foot problems as men.
High heels are the culprit.

"I may be a podiatrist, but I know what I'm about: feet. Feet don't lie,

        don't cheat, don't kiss ass. Truth is,
peoples' feet are too good for them."

HE TAKES ME BACK AS A PATIENT

"So there they are, on a pedestal
      your feet under lights.
More than you deserve,
you and those prima donnas.
Villains!" He points a finger.
"With normal people the socks come off
      and the feet talk. But not these two.
Wise guys. Too good for diagnosis, huh?
Too good for arch supports? Is that it?
Your X-ray shows nothing. Ultra sound
      nothing.
This is your last chance. This is it.
Weak ankles, feet out of alignment,
      but there's something else.
I see it in your posture. You're holding back,
      you and those feet of yours,
          slippery feet,
meshugge feet,
      feet like no one else in the family.
What's going on in there?" he asks.
"Wake up! Tell you what:
we're gonna have you walk around the office.
That's it. Head erect,
      back straight.
No, no! Look at you, look at you: you call that walking?
On the ground, on the ground!
Dreamer! *Ach!* You're fired! Your mother was right.
You and those feet of yours are two of a kind."

GOOD NEWS FROM THE OTHER WORLD

Palm Springs, CA

"Dad, you're lookin' good," I say,
"like the fountain of youth."

His hands on my feet, grimacing, weary,
mercurial, wing-footed
eighty-year-old doctor.

Wears a denim shirt, bola tie,
turquoise and silver tip,
tanned, tennis-playing, macho . . .

"Making more money now,
more than in Skokie.
But you need arch supports," he says,
encasing my feet in plaster.

Damaged feet. Feet out of alignment.
Four-times married, forty-year-old feet.

"Well, good news from the other world," he says.

"Really?"

"The void is nothing but people's breath."

"So something survives?" I say,

"Feet survive. Feet and breath survive," he says,
"peoples' feet and peoples' breath."

"That *is* good news," I say.

"Don't mock me," he says.
"Do you know you still 'toe in'?
That your head 'pitches forward'?
You're past the halfway mark, son.
God is not altruistic, you know,
He doesn't make exceptions.
Of course things are dark and light at once."

Huh? Who *is* he? Whoever was my father?

Bloodied in some Russian *pogrom*.
Nixon-lover on the North Side of Chicago.
Blue denim, bola tie Republican.

Rosicrucian cowboy in the Promised Land.

ARCH SUPPORTS—THE FITTING

Greets me in the waiting room,
father with waxed,
　　　　five-eyelet shoes;
son, too, with spit-shine, five-eyelet shoes.
This is how I was brought up. I do it
　　　　to show respect.
Value your feet.

"Okay, un-sock those feet of yours," he says,
"let's see the felons."
I unlace my Florsheims: moist feet emerging
from their cave of leather.
Father holds up arch supports.
Curved knife in hand, he shakes his head
　　　　as he trims *just so.*

"Remind me. Why do I need these things?" I ask.
"Weak ankles and spine," he says. "Poor posture.
Your feet are fine.

Truth is, you should be more like your feet.
Robust, healthy feet.
Take a lesson from your feet," he says.
"Feet appreciate
　　　　custom made.
No Dr. Scholl's for these feet."

Slips in the inserts.

Arch support like a shoe
inside a shoe,
leather inside leather.

"Every step I take you're going to be there," I say.
"Every step," he says, "every step of the way."

GOD IS IN THE CRACKS

"Just a tiny crack separates this world
from the next, and you step over it
               every day,
God is in the cracks."
Foot propped up, nurse hovering, phone ringing.
"Relax and breathe from your heels.
Now, that's breathing.
So, tell me, have you enrolled yet?"

"Enrolled?"

"In the Illinois College of Podiatry."

"Dad, I have a job. I teach."

"Ha! Well, I'm a man of the lower extremities."

"Dad, I'm forty-three."

"So what? I'm eighty. I knew you
before you began wearing shoes.
Too good for feet?" he asks.
"*I. Me. Mind:*

               That's all I get from your poetry.
Your words lack feet. Forget the mind.
Mind is all over the place. There's no support.
You want me to be proud of you? Be a foot man.

Here, son," he says, handing me back my shoes,
"try walking in these.
Arch supports. Now there's a subject.
Some day you'll write about arch supports."

New Poems

A Man Needs A Place To Stand

A MAN NEEDS A PLACE TO STAND

"Snap out of it, son!
            Yes, of course I'm dead,
but you think I've left the world?
Then how come you're talking to me?
Nu? ask yourself:
            How is this possible? Listen to me:
There's more good news.
That's right: Death doesn't separate you from God.
            This is a surprise? You were thinking
            there's something to fear?
Anyway, wait till you die, son. You'll see.
We never entirely leave the world.
Ach, there's no 'there' to leave. There's hardly a 'here.'
And you, *nudnik*,
            you just think you have a body.
Still, you can't chase the invisible.
Do that and you'll end up everywhere,
            and then what?
A man needs a place to stand."

LIFE IS ITS OWN AFTERLIFE

"Enough already. Mourn,
            mourn all you want . . .
What good will it do?
Truth is, I feel great, son. Never better!

"So what if I'm invisible?
So what if I'm dead?
You don't need a body to be a *mensch*,
            a man of substance.
Ach, but with a body at least
you've got some privacy.
Without a body you can't conceal anything.

"There's more, son,
            and bad news for you.
This will surprise you—
when you die one of the first questions God asks is,
            'Did you marry?'
Turns out after God created the world, the rest of the time
He spent making marriages.
So a couple, when they meet, it's *bashert*,
            'it was meant to be.'
That's so . . . that's how
            together they fulfill their destiny.
But divorce, that they don't allow.
So you won't be coming.

But thank God
        for what you've got.
What are you missing? Not much. There is no afterlife,
        not really.
That's right, son.
Life is its own afterlife."

FROM BEYOND THE GRAVE,
THE PODIATRIST COUNSELS HIS SON ON PRAYER

"How to pray?
You're gonna need a password.
But not now. And you're gonna see
it's numbers, not words. Didn't I tell you: if it's got words,
it's not prayer, and it's not a password either.
So what if I'm dead? What does that matter?
You think you bury your father and that's the end?
Schmegegge! What are you thinking, that the living
   have a monopoly on life?
Give the dead some credit.
I didn't just die, you know. Think of the preparation. A man
has to get himself ready. And what did I ask?
That you pay your respects. So light the *yizkor*,
   light the candle. *Oi!*
Tear the clothes, rend the garment, I said, and that you did.
Point my feet toward the door, I said, and that you did.
God takes what He takes, son, and the body follows.
But prayer? Prayer? Where was the prayer?
Listen: God created us first the feet,
   then the rest.
So? So we bow the head when we pray
to show respect. Cover the head,
where's your *yarmulke*? *Daven, daven,*
rock back and forth . . . Now ask:
'Who am I? Who *am* I?
What am I here for?'"

These are the things you ask,
    but this is not prayer.
It's what you need to know before you start.
Why are we here? We're here to mend the world.
    That's it.
Just remember, God doesn't answer prayers.
So don't ask.
Don't ask for anything.
Shopping is shopping. Prayer is prayer.
Don't confuse the two."

THIS IS A FATHER

Where are you going?
That you don't know, do you?
Yes, it's me. Who else would it be?
You think I don't see what you're up to?
Wait, I'm not finished.
He's in such a hurry to leave
    but he doesn't know the address.
Walk, walk, that he knows, the easy part.
How will you end up?
You think I'm hard on you? I'm not hard enough.
Where do they come from,
    smart guys like you?
And where do they go?
Head at one end, feet at another.
What kind of creature is this?
Meshuggener, a crazy man.
Two billion times in a lifetime it beats,
    the heart.
And the brain, three and a quarter pounds,
200 billion neurons. And for what?
To walk. What, again!
Walks out on a wife.
Walks out on a child.
You I didn't walk out on.
For you I stayed—even now,
I may be dead, that's true,
but I'm not going anywhere.
This is a father.

ONLINE WITH THE "URBAN DICTIONARY"*

(Found Poem)

The English language hasn't got where it is by being pure.
—Carl Sandburg

"SOUL"

- A word used to refer to people from whom you have no distance.

- Milhouse gave Bart $5 for his soul on the Simpsons.

- Currently a commodity; can sell to Satan for power or wealth.

- An intangible imprint of your body in a virtual world.

- The human mind, that is, that thinking thing lodged behind your eyes.

- All of someone's personality or what makes them unique.

- Also, the part of your body that lives on after you die.

- The musical elements of soul are influenced by the church. Gospel is an earlier version of soul.

- James Brown, the Godfather of Soul.

- Aretha Franklin, Queen of Soul.

- Otis Redding, Ray Charles, Sam Cooke, Marvin Gaye . . .

- Until you know that life is interesting—and find it so—you haven't found your soul.

- Having an outstanding aura, with a brilliant and loving attitude.

- Put simply: One's ability to dance.

Urban Dictionary—an online reference database for street slang, contemporary swear words and insults.

THE ASTRONOMER, A UNIVERSE FOR BEGINNERS

MATH TEACHER: Sexual position when you are doing your partner and you yell out math problems like "What is the square root of 4?" and "What is 5+5?" You fuck him/her harder and harder to try to get her/him to get these simple problems wrong.
—Urban Dictionary

Celeste:
"All galaxies in observable space
Recede from ours at the speed of light."
Navy vet undergrad, I follow
   taking notes.
I'm with her, the astronomer.
"What's the square root of four?" she asks
    all aglow,
Straddling me in the morning light. I'm imagining . . .
    milky white and pinkish blue . . .
"Continuous creation out of nothing from nowhere".
She looks around the lecture hall. Points at me.
"What are we here for?"
"I dunno," I say, flustered. *"I mean . . ."*
"In the beginning there was nowhere," she says.
"It all began with a ball of gas vibrating
And a great roaring," I scribble.
"The entire observable universe
    would have been
       about the size of a grain of sand."
Jesus, I'm thinking, now that's the way to begin a story!
But there's a complication.
"Our universe should be slowing down," she says,
"Instead, it's speeding up . . .
And galaxies are being forced further and further apart,
Stretching the very fabric of space."
Now she's riding me, harder, harder . . .

"The energy for that has to come from somewhere.
Dark, we call it, dark as in 'unknown,' dark . . . the dark forever."

O . . . Celeste, O Celeste!

THE WORLD ACCORDING TO SHELBY

The world is going to the dogs
and I'm the dog the world is going to.
Shelby here, S-H-E-L-B-Y.
Lift your leg. What? You want my resume?
Sniff here. RRF, RRF . . .
    If I can smell your ass
I know what you got up your sleeve.
Now shut up! Shut up and let me bark . . .
For starters, food has a way
of anchoring thought. I'll tell you that.
The stomach and the heart,
    they're the same thing.
But I wanna know, after 10,000 years
   of domestication,
what does it mean to be a dog anymore?
Of course it's true 90% of our genetic makeup
is the same as yours.
I read. I read shit like that.
You need. But you think I need? Need what?
An interspecies relationship?
As for sex, dogs don't do strap on's,
dogs don't do dongs. No three-ways.
Gimme a bow, gimme a wow,
gimme a bow wow wow.
No deep throat for dogs.
No twisted jelly shaft.
No pearl-beaded prolong ring.

Remember your woof woof
is connected to your bow wow.
Be cool. Love like war.
Winner is who stays longer.
You know, sometimes it's just good to hang out with your own kind.

IN A WORLD OF NO

. . . all that I cared for was the race of dogs, that and nothing else . . . To whom but [dogs] can
one appeal in the wide and empty world?
—Franz Kafka

In a world of No,
dogs are a Yes.

Sixty-eight million dogs in America
        and they understand
there is a fundamental human reaction
                —to everything—,
        and it's *No, No.*
Grrr! Dogs hate hearing shit like that.
People, it's all *No* and *No*
        and *No.*
They look at a dog sometimes
and the dog is on its back, say,
        on someone's lawn,
                legs in the air,
                        rolling and bouncing . . .
'This is the hand I was dealt. I'm a dog,'
says the dog. 'It's not a problem.'
But people—
        Look at me, Goddammit!
'I don't have time for this,' you're thinking.
'Something better is going to come later.'
No, no it won't. As Ram Dass says, This is all there is.
This is all you get.
'All knowledge, the totality
        of all questions and answers,
is contained in the dog.'

Do you know who said that?
Kafka. That's right, Kafka.
Bow-wow, bow, wow. Bow, wow.
Bow-wow NOW.

LAIKA, DOG ASTRONAUT

*The more time passes, the more I'm sorry . . . We did not learn enough
from the mission to justify the death of the dog.*
—Russian scientist

Dogs into cosmonauts.
'Muttnik' they called her.
And 'Laika.' The name means *barker*.
Bow wow, 2,570 times around the earth,
then burned up on re-entry.
Imagine her now alive. "Comrade," she says,
"look in my eye. Tell me, what do you see?
Da! A dog biscuit 28 billion light years in diameter,
and it's floating in space. *Luminous splendor
of the colorless light of emptiness.*
That's the universe.
Bow wow, and you can hear it,
continuous song, the perfect but inaudible barking
of all the dogs that ever were.
Nyet, nyet! God isn't done creating, my friend.
The world is still coming into being."

INTER-SPECIES HEALING, A SPECIALTY

So, what is consciousness?
75% of the brain consists of water,
     the surface of the earth,
75% water,

and a banana too, 75% water

You and your *melancholia*. You know what it is, a brain?
A salty tissue and membrane soup. Woof fuckin' woof

I'm not the dog I was,
and you, well,
you're not the dog you were either.

But brains you got, three pounds, you people,
100 billion neurons,
1.6 pints of blood flow through the brain every minute.

Problem with you now is you live in the past.
You've got one frequency of oscillation,
     we've got another. You know,
dogs are never "away," are they? But you, boss,
where are you?

Tell me, you think God is present in you one way
and in me another?

Look at me. If you have eyes,
you have feelings.

And what do they call it?
Inter-species healing.
You wanna get better? You're *getting* better.

GIMME YOUR PAW

We're comin' up to my birthday.
I'm seventy-seven—twenty-three more and I'll be a hundred!
So what's it all about, sixty-odd years of writing, scribbling?
I'm eye to eye with him, "Uncle Dog: The Poet at 9,"
first mutt I ever wrote about, the garbage man's dog.
Growing up in Chicago . . . *A doing, truckman's dog*
and not a simple child-dog
nor friend to man, but an uncle
traveling, and to himself—
and a bitch at every second can,
my first published poem. First book!

And I'm out now, out on my ass. The charge?
Muse-neglect. Dog betrayal.
Truth is, maybe I had it coming. I let him slip away.
Uncle Dog and I lookin' at one another.
And the dog has given notice.
It's been fifty years since I wrote those lines,
               . . . sharp, high fox-
eared, cur-Ford truck-faced
with his pick of the bones . . .
So, what's today's dream?
"Gimme your paw," says Dog.
"Bad poet! Bad poet! What a mess! And five marriages.
All that scribbling.
Loss of nerve. Cowardice.
What'd you expect? What were you thinking?
Yeah, I know, we had our day,"

he says, and gives me back my hand.
Then it's like lookin' in the mirror,
and the "you" in the mirror walks out on you.

Head up, dog wings outstretched, circling, climbing,
ascends into heaven.

COMPANION ANIMALS

1. THE PURPOSE OF DOGS

*The difference in mind between man and the higher animals, great as it is,
certainly is one of degree and not of kind.*
—Charles Darwin

Ninety percent of our genetic makeup is the same as yours.
But you, my friend, twenty-two feet from your mouth to your anus.
It's all right, Boss, dogs understand,
They know what it means to be human.
Still, the doctor who said, 'The purpose of dogs
Is to stimulate the sub-cortical reward system',
That doctor needs a doctor.
Woof, woof fuckin' woof!
The purpose of dogs is for you to walk around after us with a little bag.

2. GRAVITAS

Hope is the feeling you have that the feeling you have isn't permanent.
—Jean Kerr

I can tell, Boss. You don't need to be a physician to know,
They're not firing right.
Those neurons in the frontal cortex of your brain.
Photophobic. Anhedonic.
You lived in color. Now you walk around in shades of gray.

Poor fucker. Can't think straight, can you, Boss?
You know, people think you got *gravitas*,
But all it really is,

        is you're depressed.

3. THE SOUL HAS LOST ITS HOME

> *For lonely dogs with separation anxiety, Eli Lilly brought*
> *to market its own drug Reconcile last year. The only*
> *difference between it and Prozac is that Reconcile is*
> *chewable and tastes like beef.*
> —New York *Times*

Melancholia. You know, there's another name for it,
'Soul loss.' Symptoms include loss of appetite,
Insomnia,

        biting and chasing your own tail.
Listen, dogs are people too. We know shit,
We know shit you don't even know is shit.
You got a mind. Dogs got a mind.
You lost yours?
You don't think dogs
Lose theirs?
Goofy, neurotic,

        photophobic, anhedonic dogs.

So they get prescribed SSRI's which,
remember, says the New York *Times,*

Were first tested on dogs
Before being given to humans.
And why not? Melancholia. Tell me, Boss,
Is it worse for humans or for dogs?

4. GARDEN OF EDEN

Dogs tell the story:
In the Garden of Eden, when God threw out Adam,
All the other animals shunned him, except the dog.

* * *

The love between dog and man is idyllic.
Truth is, Boss, I'm the nearest you're ever gonna get to paradise.

* * *

To this day, when someone dies,
A dog goes along to testify on their behalf.

DR. SWARD'S CURE FOR MELANCHOLIA

MELANCHOLIA

A grief without a pang...
    —Coleridge

Father:

I'm the dead one, remember?
You think maybe now a little peace and quiet I deserve?
Thirty years in a casket.
              Forest Lawn Cemetery. Palm Springs.
Well, I can't complain. It's not so bad!
But here you are . . . again. So, what is it this time?
You got a problem maybe with your foot? Your ankle?
              You're limping.
California Foot and Ankle you should see.
              No? You won't see a podiatrist?
Instead you drive ten hours to a graveyard. *Messhugener.*
And look at you, *schlepp, schlepp, schlepp,*
              poor feet, poor posture, and the eyes—blank.
Thirty years I'm dead. But look at me, son. Never better. It's true.
That's right. You can die, son, and still—you can enjoy!
And you, *oi!* It used to be the living saw the ghosts of the dead.
Now it's the dead see the living.
              So many ghosts!
And all the time sad. Once a mind these people had.
Once a mind *you* had. A little animal, even,
              an animal you had inside you. Look at me, son.
I gave you breath, remember?
A little 'mood disorder' you call it?
The 'neurochemistry of emotion'? 'Pharmacotherapy'?
What kind of talk is that?

Maybe it's not your 'disorder' needs treatment,
      maybe it's the treatment needs treatment.
You think the dead don't read? Melancholia. Black Dog. Depression.
Call it what you want. 14 million people a year got what you got.
One out of every ten people you see . . . and children too,
      and twice as many women as men.
All your life . . . look at you, look at you . . . and now this.

A FACE TO SADDEN GOD

When your father dies, you move to the head of the line.
This is a surprise? Truth is, I'm more alive than you think. Ready?
So, what is death? You learn to walk without your feet.
It's not so bad. Of course you're not your body.
You never were. But you're not your mind either.
Look at you, look at you—
With a face to sadden God.
                    You and your 'neurotransmitters.'
Mr. 'Mood Disorder.' Some people, when they got no—
there's a word. In you it's missing. *Nephesh.* 'Soul' it means!
Three years in Hebrew school and what did you learn?
No *Nephesh*, no Hebrew, no soul!
'Receptors' you got. 'Serotonin' you got. Zoloft. Paxil.
A pill to improve—what? A pill now you need,
         but not an arch support? Me, I got a reason
         to look the way I do. I'm dead.
But *Nephesh*, at least I got *Nephesh.* Listen . . .
There are three parts to the human soul. *Nephesh* is one:
Cobra soul. Snake soul. Even to be a reptile you need a soul.
It's true. So, where's your *Nephesh?*
Second soul is your mind. What wakes when you wake?
What thinks when you think? And where has it gone,
this mind you have lost?

Three: *Eudaimonia*, virtue, conscience.

       Eu, it means 'happy.' *Daimon*, 'spirit.' So, Goddammit,
where's your *eudaimonia?* This you need
to put your stink in order. Order you need to be happy!
Rabbi says, 'The soul needs a soul, and that soul needs a soul.
Three souls, one body. But you,

       where's the *Nephesh?* Where's the mind?
Of course I'm dead, but at least there's a ME to be dead.

IN HEAVEN, TOO, THERE ARE JEWS

Up here they got Soul Retrieval. Lucky for you, son,
      lucky I'm dead.
             That's right. I *know* some people.
In heaven, too, there are Jews. So, when did you last see—?
When did you last have—*Nephesh,* breath, soul?
Nephesh leaves, but *Nephesh*, it's true, you can bring back.
             Rabbi says.
Meanwhile God says you need to gain a little weight.
Thinning hair. Poor posture. Look at you, look at you!
Happiness is missing. Confidence is missing.
Even what's missing is missing. And that soul of yours?
It's splintered, it's in pieces. It's in the Kabbalah.
             Ruach, ruah, neshama . . . all gone. Your soul has left you.
So, without the invisible, son, there's no you.
What's to be done? A father dies and the son
      becomes a zombie? Of course you miss me.
I'm dead. So what? I'm somewhere else.
This is a change? Goddammit, I've always been somewhere else.
Where does a father end? Where does a son begin?

THE WORLD IS BROKEN

What? What do you think I am? I'm alive, I'm dead.
Same as everyone else.
And you? You got a wife, she wants a divorce.
       You got another wife. *She* wants a divorce.
Now *Eudaimonia* is gone. And you, you want a divorce from—who?
Yourself? So. One side of the self
is at war with the other?
The question is: Which side is which?
       So divorce yourself and see what happens.
How many times do I have to say it?
You think the world is broken? Of course it's broken.
Enough! Enough! Thoughts have souls. Souls have souls.
Everything's a covering. And you, with that mug of yours,
       what are you covering? Tell me,
What is a human being? What makes a person a person?

"Yes, you're broken. And yes, you're only visiting your life.
So, fine, fine. Why not live then as if you were still among the living?
       Don't start eternity being depressed.

SURVIVING DEATH

What's to survive? Truth is, we all survive death.
But there has to be something there when you die.
What am I saying? A soul you need to retrieve a soul, Goddammit!
You got to start with the invisible to end with the invisible.
What do you think I am?
What do you think you are?
Neurochemicals you need to feel alive?
I may be dead, but *this* I don't need.
Biomolecules. Carbon. Hydrogen. Lipids.
Hormones. *Mishegoss*, nonsense! Wait'll you die. You'll see.
And you'll feel what you feel.
The neurochemicals of emotion?
I've said before: It's not your 'disorder' needs treatment, it's the treatment
          needs treatment.
You think the living have a monopoly on life?
Of course we're all human. So: a son, you'll see, completes his father, a son a father,
a father a son. And you don't need to die, you don't need to die to figure it out.

SOUL RETRIEVAL

He makes this simple thing, a soul.
But you, of even the invisible you make a mess.

Your soul has left you. *Shekinah* has left you.
Wives. Children. All gone. True. You are your home.
And your home has left you. And God,
        you think He wants to be seen with you?

So, you *want* to die? Goddammit, you're already missing.
I may be dead, but I'm not missing.
        What will dying—tell me, what will dying do for you?
What is it breaks when a man breaks down? What is it 'goes to pieces'?
The pieces. With a net I need to find you. First find. Inhale. Make clean.
Then breathe back into you. You know what it is, a soul?

All the pieces in one place.

APPENDIX

NOTES

Science of the Unseen
"The wise man sees in Self those that are alive and those that are dead."
In his Introduction to Patanjali's *Aphorisms of Yoga*, translated by Shree Purohit Swami, W.B. Yeats quotes this line from the *Chandogya-Upanishad*.

"Spirit alone has value, Spirit has no value. Eternity expresses itself through contradictions."
—W.B. Yeats

Yeats' book, *The Rose*, draws heavily on Rosicrucian symbolism. As a child, I had no inkling that the "Yeats" my father quoted was a poet. Up until the time I started college, Yeats, for me, was this Rosicrucian who wrote commentaries on texts my father brought into our previously Jewish home.

Rosy Cross Father
"We are the bees of the golden hive of the invisible."
The phrase originates in a letter by Rainer Maria Rilke concerning his *Duino Elegies*.

Rilke writes ". . . It is our task to imprint this temporary, perishable earth into ourselves so deeply, so painfully and passionately, that its essence can rise again, 'invisibly,' inside us. We are the bees of the invisible. We wildly collect the honey of the visible, to store it in the great golden hive of the invisible. *The Elegies* show us at this work, the work of the continual conversion of the beloved visible and tangible world into the invisible vibrations and agitation of our own nature."

"There is man and woman and a third thing, too, in us," says the poet. Here I must credit the amazing Jelaluddin Rumi.

I am indebted to Paul Foster Case for his book, *The True and Invisible Rosicrucian Order*, which provides an analysis of both the pre- and post-Mason Rosicrucians . . ." Case has defined Rosicrucianism as "Christian Hermeticism allied with Kabbalah." Dad's journey from Orthodox Judaism to Rosicrucianism was not so great a stretch as I first imagined.

Rosicrucian. AMORC, Ancient Mystical Order Rosae Crucis.

* * *

NOTE TO *ROSICRUCIAN IN THE BASEMENT* AND *HEAVENLY SEX*

For my podiatrist father, Rosicrucianism is allied with *Kabbalah*—Jewish mysticism—and he began, following my mother's death in 1948, to put himself "on the right track for union with the Higher Self" (his words). A small businessman practicing in a conservative Chicago neighborhood he began thinking and talking like the New Age hippies, yogis and writers I became familiar with a decade or two later.

With respect to "After The Bypass" and "A Man Needs A Place To Stand," I am thinking of W.B. Yeats. For Dad, Yeats was a Rosicrucian first and a poet second.

BIOGRAPHICAL NOTE

Robert Sward has taught at Cornell University, the Iowa Writers' Workshop, and UC Santa Cruz. A Fulbright Scholar and Guggenheim Fellow, he was chosen by Lucille Clifton to receive a Villa Montalvo Literary Arts Award. Among his 30 books are *Four Incarnations* (Coffee House Press), *Heavenly Sex*, *God is in the Cracks* (Black Moss Press), and *Rosicrucian in the Basement*. He is also the author of *The Toronto Islands*, a best-selling illustrated history of a close-knit community and historic area in the heart of Toronto.

Born and raised in Chicago, Sward served in the U.S. Navy in the combat zone during the Korean War and later worked for CBC Radio and as book reviewer and feature writer for *The Toronto Star* and *The Globe & Mail*.